a *Kingdom of Slaves* book

The Slave Palace
Wulf and Locke

by

Wendy Rathbone

Acknowledgments

I'd like to give a special thanks to **Della Van Hise** for this book's stunningly gorgeous cover.

Also, a thousand thank yous to **Christina E. Pilz** for a wonderful beta-read of this novel.

And last but best of all, another thank you to my partner **Della Van Hise** for help with formatting and uploading my books. I couldn't do this without you.

A Teensy Bit of Background Before You Start

The **Kingdom of Slaves** series of standalone novels is set in a contemporary, fantasy version of Earth, present day, where the selling and owning of pleasure slaves is legal in most countries.

Avilan is the largest and wealthiest country in the contemporary world. It has three hundred and twenty-one slave palaces. But the largest and greatest sits in the center of the capital city of Lirangel. The palace has its own helicopter pad, security force, computer internet, hospital, mall, and small college.

There is no king of the Slave Palace. It is run by a board of trainers. The highest trainers, known as Eminent Masters, over-see all. They form a board of trustees who maintain the palace economy, its rules, and its ways.

The Slave Palaces produce Avilan's largest commodity. Pleasure slaves. While anyone may own a pleasure slave, only the truly wealthy can afford Slave Palace trained slaves.

Untrained slaves are bought and sold in the marketplace every day. Some offer themselves willingly to be trained. Some are in financial trouble, or are criminals. Some are prisoners of war. The more violent offenders considered dangerous are sold as One-Night Thralls, meant to be sexually used in any way the owner decides before they are put down for the good of society.

While societal rules demand pleasure slaves never be permanently harmed, One-Night Thralls are not subject to this law. It is, in fact, Avilan's version of a death penalty.

Chapter One – Locke

"Parcival never cuts corners, I'll give him that," Malik said.

Locke looked up at the towering building before him. *New Venture Hotel.*

Not all pleasure slave brokers from the streets of Lirangel, the capitol of Avilan, were the same. Parcival had the best reputation for acquiring and dealing in the cleaner sorts. They included those who had nowhere else to go, or who were in extreme debt, but weren't exactly criminals, addicts, or carriers of diseases and STDs most people in the civilized world had been vaccinated against.

All of Parcival's slaves were completely willing, choosing to give themselves over to training instead of going to prison, or in the case of debtors, to camps where they worked menial labor until their debts were paid.

As an Eminent Master, Locke bought slaves from Parcival fairly consistently, and brought them to the Slave Palace to be trained and sold.

The Slave Palace had just finished another round of its own auctions, and again there were rooms to be filled.

"Yes." Locke agreed. "A high-end meal. A free bar. Today he's selling at the hotel's wedding garden. The weather is perfect. He certainly treats his customers well."

There were slave brokers who dealt out of musty bars or smoky backrooms in tenements and warehouses. Locke had found some gems in those places, but he detested that scene. But this! This was more like it. And one of the better perks of his job.

As Locke and Malik entered the hotel lobby, cool air wafted over their faces. It had a faint floral scent, clean and regulated.

Lavish couches and lamps decorated the lobby. The floor was terracotta, pretty but not as luxurious as the Palace's marble decor. Still, the hotel sat in the nicer section of downtown. The humming song of the casino to the right thrummed in his ears. Much as Locke enjoyed gambling, that was not where he was headed today.

A sign at the front of the lobby greeted them.

Parcival's Extraordinary Slave Auction 2pm – 4pm.
Main Wedding Garden

Beneath the words, a large red arrow pointed the direction.

Locke and Malik found their way easily. They'd both been to the New Venture many times.

When they came to the garden entrance, a man in a black tuxedo with white gloves and a top hat took their entry tickets. A woman in a black suit and red tie then greeted them and showed them to their seats.

Today everything was arranged like a formal banquet with tables sporting lacy white cloths, chairs with tall backs, and fondue fountains in the center of every set-up.

Locke and Malik were given the choicest table, center-front, with the best view of the small white stage where weddings were performed, and on off-days, where slaves were sold.

Malik smiled and rolled his eyes. "Oh my, I'm already bored."

Locke laughed. It was true Malik was jaded, but he was much more of a snob than Locke. He liked being spoiled. And he had a sadistic streak, enjoying the trembling and fear of new slaves who had no idea what was coming next for them.

While Eminent Masters did not partake in training sessions as often as regular daily trainers, what with all the paperwork and meetings required to run the Palace, they were allowed to take on choice projects. They wouldn't be Eminent Masters if they did not enjoy their work. And they were the best at what they did.

Malik was not an Eminent Master, and still trained slaves every day. Locke preferred to oversee general training, and had not taken on a personal trainee in over a year. Neither Malik nor Locke were as bored or jaded as they often pretended to be.

While they waited for the show to begin, Locke ordered white wine. Malik had a martini, shaken-not-stirred. He'd been a Bond fan from way back. He even spoke with a posh Bond accent, although it was faked. He'd perfected it back when they were in college together. These days, Locke was the only person who knew the accent was not authentic.

More guests arrived. Wealthy businessmen and women, mostly, or freelance trainers looking for stock. Locke recognized two. They didn't directly compete in business with the Palace, but they did all right for themselves selling trained slaves to the middle class.

As long as your credit was good, Parcival did not care who he sold to.

When the tables were full, appetizers came. The caterers kept the plates coming. Green salad. Vegetable soup. Quail. Red potatoes. Fresh sourdough rolls.

Locke ate little. He mostly enjoyed his wine. And waited for the main attraction.

Chapter Two - Wulf

Wulf fought harder than he ever had in his life. But it was already too late. The chains were too thick. If he hadn't been bruised and exhausted, he might've outrun the slavers.

Slavers.

For that was what they were. Not soldiers as they called themselves. Not operatives. Not people who were trained in the dignity and art of being a warrior as Wulf was. No. Wulf had learned from school-age on, these were thugs. Kidnappers. And all they cared about was profit.

Oh, they claimed Wulf's country of Rille was an enemy to Avilan, that Rille sent terrorists to Avilan to do unspeakable deeds. Wulf had been taught this was propaganda. The truth as he knew it was all Avilan wanted when they came to another country to fight was new bodies to enslave and torture.

Commander Auffit had taught all the men and women in Wulf's unit well. Told them all of the evils of Avilan. Of the debauchery in the streets. The sex fiends that ran the country. Avilan citizens had no respect for themselves, or the sanctity of marriage and monogamy. Or the purity of virginity. Their actions were impure. Evil. He taught that Rille was a victim of the wealth and greed of a country filled with devils. All the lies and gossips about terrorists from Rille were an excuse for Avilan slavers to come into their little country and steal its citizens for profit and gain. Take them and make them into slaves. Pleasure slaves.

What a concept! It was sick. Twisted. Wrong.

But now Wulf was caught.

Well, if there was nothing more for him than this, he could at least go down fighting. And maybe take a few of these evil bastards with him.

Even chained, he had options. Strength. Force. Weight. He'd trained hard, learned that a fight never really ended. One could pretend to surrender, then play the long game. He would observe, distract, deflect. Wait for his moment.

The slavers used box trucks with benches in the back to transport their prisoners to their base camp.

As two men shoved Wulf into the back of a truck at gunpoint, one said to the other, "Watch that one. He went ape-shit on Bax. Broke his arm. And Pontrose is still unconscious in the med van."

"What happened?"

"Crazy mother-fucker. That's what happened."

Wulf had only defended himself. He wasn't crazy. He was proud of the fact that it took half a dozen slavers to take him down and chain him. Gag him. It wasn't just his size that intimidated. He knew precise moves. He'd practiced to be a warrior for his people since he was ten years old. It was all he could think to do to gain the approval of a cruel father. He moved fast. He thought fast. He had never lost a fight.

"He's a big one, I'll give him that."

Now the man who spoke turned his full attention onto Wulf.

"Hey, giant!"

Wulf glared, every muscle in his body tense, ready. The gag in his mouth tightened as he tried to sneer.

"Don't you know," the guy continued, "that you're going to a better life?" Then he laughed. "What are you afraid of? Because you fought so hard, me and the guys here decided you won't go to an ordinary prison." He held out a tablet with some writing on it. "See here? We forged your papers with our signature saying you volunteered to be sold to the pleasure farms. You'll be sold, trained, then sold again. All for pleasure. You'll be taken good care of. It'll be a nice royalty for us. A guy with your looks and muscles will go for a pretty penny. You'll want for nothing."

Wulf wanted to scream. All he could manage was a muffled cough. These men were depraved, evil. Did they not know the sanctity of the body was everything? Did they have no shame? No sense of honor for the temple that encased human life?

Obviously not. Avilanians had no souls.

Avilan, Kingdom of Slaves, forced its ways upon the world. Besmirched the purity of the soul. Fighting them was his job. He had no other purpose.

The back door to the truck slid shut on blue sky stained with smoke, a city burnt and ruined, the black silhouettes of dead trees along a range of mountains that turned purple at dusk.

This was what Avilan did to countries that disagreed with their ways and fought them. He'd been told this. Now he saw it firsthand.

Wulf's last glimpse of his only home and the sacred lands he'd grown up in faded to darkness.

Chapter Three – Locke

Parcival, a short round man with tight red curls on the top of his head, took center stage.

He wore a pinstripe suit that almost fit, and when he opened his mouth he sounded like a carnival barker.

"Ladies and Gentlemen. Welcome, welcome! All gather to see the greatest of slave stock, gathered from far exotic locales and as close to home as your own native city. Here you will find the tightest of virgins, the most obedient of servants, those looking to please and tease you, the shiniest, the prettiest, the finest in breeding, the strongest in stature. These slaves I am about to show you are untrained, it is true, but they are waiting to be molded by your very hands and minds, waiting to become the finest in pleasure you will ever know."

It was almost the truth. Parcival got his slaves the same way the seedier brokers did, by wholesale buying debtor contracts or the signed deeds of white collar criminals, or wheeling and dealing with the military for their prisoners of war. Or perhaps he even partook in the illegal gain of kidnapping by way of organized crime. Most brokers did. He simply liked to put on more of a show, and spent extra to show off his harems.

Locke leaned back in his chair and sipped his wine.

When Parcival was done with his opening speech, he waved at a curtained doorway to the left and behind the stage. The black velvet curtain shimmied. Something sharp poked it. Finally, it opened.

A line of female slaves entered the room, all loosely chained in faux gold, their wrists bound, their necks collared.

The women always entered first in Parcival's shows. Naked and young. Wide-eyed and shy. Not the lewd sorts that came from backrooms on the seedier side of town. These were sold as true virgins, but Locke still doubted it. Where they came from — their histories — would all be in their paperwork. But for now, everything was about comportment, looks and health.

To Locke they all looked far too skinny. But that could easily be remedied at the Palace where they would be served scheduled, balanced meals.

Malik liked women better than men, so he would be the one to acquire the females today.

Locke waited for the men. His forte was in training the males. They were often more stubborn and had a fight in them, but he enjoyed the challenge. And physically, he preferred them, their tight-muscled bodies, their hard cocks. Though he could take on female charges as well, and do the job, he'd always enjoyed the males the most.

Malik took his time choosing who to bid on from the female line-up. He went onto the stage and examined close-up several of the slaves he would bid on.

Satisfied, he came back to his seat.

"I'll be bidding on at least four," he commented.

Locke nodded, saying nothing.

The men came next, and there were twice as many of them as there were females.

Locke put his wine glass down and sat up.

The first to cross the white wedding stage was a gorgeous youth with good confirmation and a big cock. The large nametag he wore around his neck said he was called Zale. Already, Locke knew from the man's appearance that Zale would do well at the Palace.

When Locke was a new trainer, still wet behind the ears, he took his laptop on buying excursions and made copious notes. Now as an Eminent Master, he knew pretty much at first glance who he was getting right away. He rarely went onto the stage to examine the prospects. And he memorized names easily.

This first one, Zale, was a beauty.

Two buyers approached Zale, handled him politely, then went back to their seats.

The same routine occurred for the next twenty-three slaves.

Locke made a mental note of six he would bid on before Malik leaned toward him and whispered, "You're far too nonchalant today. Do you see nothing that intrigues you?"

"They all intrigue me." Locke turned to look at his friend. "They all have stories, probably sad ones. But we only have room for so many."

"Yes, but you look far too bored. Don't tell me you're becoming like me, jaded and old."

Locke chuckled. "You're old at 35? That's pathetic."

"You're only a year younger than me."

"No, I'm not bored. I just... the routines are all pretty much the same. I know my job and I do it."

"Yes, my dear, as I said," Malik replied. "Bored."

After the men had walked off to wait with the women behind the curtain for the auction to begin, Parcival came back to the stage.

"There is one last special item. I usually leave these items to the street dealers, but this one was too magnificent to pass up. Wulf is an acquisition I was lucky to come across from Avilan's very own Special Forces unit. He's from our enemy country, Rille, home to terrorist regimes to numerous to list and recently conquered as you have probably seen from every social media news source in existence. He is a trained warrior and was able to take down two Special Forces officers while chained and drugged. They both almost died. He is an amazing physical specimen of humanity, a beauty unclaimed, too dangerous to train, and it is such a waste that he must be put down. But before that happens, he is on the docket to be sold as a One-Night Thrall. All rules for the handling and fair treatment of slaves are forfeit with Wulf. I'm sure you all have customers on the side who favor this sort of item, so the bids on him will go high."

Parcival turned to the left of the stage. "So without further adieu, I give you Wulf!"

The curtain parted and a large man in thick chains from ankles to neck, stumbled onto the garden path beside the stage.

Locke's muscles tensed upon seeing this man. He was indeed magnificent. Beneath the bruises and cuts on his arms and legs, he was golden in hue, smooth, with very little body hair. It took four handlers to shove him forward, two with their guns drawn. Wulf's muscles bulged as he fought against the pushes. His head turned right to left, jerking, and his golden hair fell into his eyes and against the red ball-gag that filled his mouth.

The chains rattled. The man's impressive cock swung side to side as he struggled to stay upright while still fighting his captors right up to the side of the stage.

Locke calculated that if this man was from Rille, he'd already spent nearly a whole day on a flight to Avilan. And before that, he'd probably been held in a military prison for who knew how long. Days? Weeks?

Yet the only wear and tear he showed was bruising and scrapes. His eyes, a brilliant blue, were wide and unflinching. The whites were bright and healthy, unmarred. He looked like he still retained the strength to barrel through a wall.

"Who'd have guessed Parcival would come up with this as his final auction item?" Malik whispered. "A One-Night Thrall."

"Parcival's outdone himself this time," replied Locke. His eyes never left the creature in front of him. He was close enough that he could smell him, the sweat of anger and fear, the salt essence of a man who knew he was on the way to the gallows and wasn't going to make it easy on the ones leading him there.

Malik chuckled. "Still bored?"

"Not in the least."

"Well, it's entertainment, I'll give Parcival that."

Several people were already lined up to examine the specimen before the slave even climbed the two steps to the stage.

Locke didn't realize his mouth was open until Malik gave him a friendly smack on the shoulder.

"Want to go up there and see him for yourself?"

Locke finally looked away. "No."

But he couldn't understand himself in this moment. His heart hammered in his chest. His stomach filled with little shivers.

Locke had come far in his job. He had been doing this for fourteen years, two of them as an apprentice trainer. Now he was an Eminent Master. He'd learned to keep his emotions at bay.

The hardest lesson was to enjoy his work but keep himself distant at the same time. Trainers who found that perfect middle ground produced exceptional slaves which went for high dollar amounts. Slaves responded to reward and affection, but keeping a slave from imprinting on a master was what it was all about. You couldn't be too cold, but you couldn't be too hot, either.

Right now, Locke was feeling the heat. He watched as potential buyers handled the merchandise, some simply feeling the tenseness of his bulging muscles, others crudely examining his ass, testing the weight of his balls.

Hands gripped the man's cock, squeezing not so nicely which was against the usual rules, and the pain of it put Wulf into a tight rage. He pushed forward all of a sudden, scattering the buyers, and half-fell off the stage before his four handlers could even react.

At the front and center table, Locke was up from his chair in seconds, catching the weight of the man against his chest and shoulder, holding him upright.

Hot. So hot to the touch.

"There now," Locke said. "These tiles are hard on the knees."

Wulf tossed his head forward, then back. His tangles of hair nearly hit Locke in the face. His bright eyes met Locke's for a second, then the gaze twisted away and the man tried to say something behind his gag.

"Got your balance?" Locke said calmly.

The blue eyes sought his again. The golden brows narrowed.

"All right, then," said Locke, and he moved back and sat down in his chair which put his eyes level with the enemy warrior's hips and impressive genitalia.

The handlers surrounded Wulf and forced him back behind the stage and the velvet curtain.

Malik leaned forward, handing Locke a newly filled glass of wine.

Locke took it and drank a deep mouthful.

"What was that about?" Malik asked.

"He was about to hurt himself. Parcival had a lack in common sense bringing him here."

"Well, it's all business." Malik picked up his own drink and clinked his glass to Locke's.

"Yes. Yes it is."

But Locke's palm was still tingling where it had impacted with Wulf's arm. And that body against his chest. The weight of it. The fiery energy. All amazing.

The tremors in Locke's stomach threatened to move lower.

Chapter Four – Wulf

The plane trip to Avilan could only be described as a nightmare. Wulf, separated from the other prisoners, continued to fight his handlers.

They had bound him and that still didn't keep him from butting against their bodies with his own, so for his journey to the airstrip, and the duration of the flight, they put him in a straitjacket, bound his ankles, and wheeled him in a sort of upright chair into the cargo hold.

From there they transferred him to a cage where he had room only to curl up on the floor with his knees to his chest. He did not have any space to stretch out. If he sat up, his head hit the cage's top.

Someone had affixed a container of water to the side of the cage with a strange, curving metal straw. Luckily, they'd taken away his gag. He found he could suck water from that straw. But as for food, there was none. His last meal had been offered to him in the prison, and he'd ignored it as he had all other meals for two days.

The floor of the cargo hold rumbled. It was cold. But the sound and the slight vibration finally put him to sleep. Only to have him startle awake at every bit of turbulence the plane hit.

Off and on, for twenty-three hours, this confinement was Wulf's entire world.

The cold grew worse after a while. He had on only the straitjacket and a pair of gray coveralls which protected him not at all.

When the plane finally landed and his guards hauled him from the cage, his muscles cramped. His entire body began to shake. He could barely stand.

Luckily, he didn't have to. The funny wheelchair became his mode of conveyance, for his handlers could not trust him.

He wanted to laugh at that notion for he had no strength left, but more, he wanted to cry.

The prisoners transported with him on the flight were strangers to him. His fellow warriors in his unit were gone. He'd seen them all taken down. Why he had remained unscathed, he did not know, for there were no gods looking out for him anymore, nothing left. The damned Avilanians took everything from him and now all he had was death. He decided he wanted it. He was ready to embrace it.

Wulf was taken to another holding cell, allowed to use the toilet with the straitjacket still in place, and given injections. He first thought the injections were drugs but when he started to feel more energized, decided they were some sort of vitamin supplement to keep him going.

A group of men and women came by his cell, all in suits, and peered in at him, then left.

Later, he was taken from the cell and put, still bound at the ankles and in the straitjacket, into a van and driven to some unknown destination. The drive lasted far into the night. He endured more hours of muscle cramping and bound limbs.

His stomach growled. He ignored it.

When the van finally stopped, he was strangely grateful. As he was hauled outside, deft hands removed his gag.

He did not yell or scream. All he wanted as to gulp the fresh, cool air. He stretched his legs. He longed to come out of the straitjacket, and even thought about saying he would cooperate now, but kept his mouth shut.

He could not forget the cold ruined city he'd left behind, or his dead comrades who had fought and slept by him side to side. When Avilan went to war against its enemies, they obviously left little to nothing standing in their wake.

Now Wulf stood in a shadowed alleyway, the pavement damp under his bare feet. He smelled rain in the air though none fell, and saw puddles flashing in dim light coming from a main street at the mouth of the alley.

He had had the van all to himself, but now as more vans pulled up he saw other humans pulled from the backs of the vehicles, all chained as he was except for the straitjacket.

Black-clad men herded the people altogether and led them into a set of rusted double doors.

Inside, the warehouse air smelled dank and dusty. The ceiling was at least two floors high and sported flickering fluorescent lights that sent the interior into a scuttling of shadows.

The air seemed more frigid inside than out.

Despite the temperature, the guards stripped all the chained humans of their clothing.

Wulf was turned roughly. He felt a gun put this temple, and gravelly voice said, "If you try anything, you're dead."

People surrounded him. Hands removed his straitjacket and knives were used to cut away his coverall. Now he stood naked and shivering, hands manacled in front, ankles chained to his hands.

Someone slapped him on the rear. "Turn!"

He found himself in a line up of naked, chained prisoners. Instantly, his mind counted them. Ten in all, including himself, stood before a group of guards.

A short man in a suit came in through the rusted doors.

"What've you got? And dammit, why are you calling me past midnight?"

"They need to be moved," one of the men said. "We have nowhere to put them all. Fifty k for the lot."

"For this ragtag bunch? Twenty, no more. And even so, some of them don't look at all healthy."

The haggling continued. Wulf stared at the man with the money. Small. Pale. He could crush him under one foot.

Finally, the guards forced them to move out a set of new doors and into more vans.

When Wulf reached the outside, he body-shoved one of the guards hard.

Guns came up aimed at his chest and head.

"Is this one trouble?" the small man asked.

"Could be. But he's a looker. He'd get you a fortune even if he has to be put down after."

"Dammit, Sy, are you fucking me over?"

"Why would I? You're my favorite broker, Parcival."

Wulf ended up in a new van for another long drive.

His second destination was another cell. But this time he shard it with nine others, all naked, all chained at the ankles and wrists.

In the cell was a single toilet and rudimentary shower. The guards instructed them to "be clean by tomorrow or else."

While most of the prisoners were frightened, and sought to get to know each other for comfort, Wulf spent his waking time looking for a way out. He ignored all overtures of friendship, for he could not afford to be responsible for anyone else if he were to escape.

By morning, everyone but Wulf had showered. They'd eaten. They'd memorized each other's names. Wulf had not.

The guards opened the cell door and everyone filed out. Wulf was the last.

"Did you not understand the orders to be clean?"

Wulf replied, "I did."

"You're filthy."

Wulf brought his chained hands up hard, bloodying the guard's nose.

More guards came running.

Wulf stood quietly, watching with some satisfaction the blood run down the injured guard's lips and chin. He startled when the muzzle of a gun smacked him hard just under the side of his head.

A ringing began in his ears.

"Into the shower. Now!" Hands pushed him back into the cell. Another guard came in and turned on the water to the open shower.

More guards pushed him under the cold stream.

Wulf yelled, tossed his head. The water streamed over him.

Hands held him all over. The water came at him like sleet. More hands, slippery with liquid soap, ran all over his body. He heard laughter. He clenched his teeth so hard he thought his jaw would pop.

The hands went everywhere. Someone commented, "Look at his junk. It's huge."

Fingers squeezed his cock, hurting him. More fingers drew down his crack, soaping him, grabbing his balls from behind. Making his muscles tense until they ached.

Wulf cried out.

Something struck him in the stomach. He bent over in pain.

"There! Now! While he's bent over, get his hair."

More of the soapy liquid was poured over his head. Fingers tugged and pulled at his hair until tears backed up behind Wulf's closed eyes.

When they were done cleaning him, they didn't even dry him off. He was paraded outside soaked and freezing, and tossed along with the others into a van with benches lining the sides.

Wulf sat, head bowed, damp hair trailing across his shoulders and in his eyes.

Someone to his left, a female, said, "It makes it harder when you fight, doesn't it?"

Wulf refused to answer. How could anyone give into this? He would rather die. Then he remembered what the slaver had said to him back in Rille. That they'd forged permission papers from Wulf. Did that mean people actually willingly gave permission to be handled in this way? To be sold? To be trained as sex slaves?

The van stopped and this time they were let out onto a sunny alley with asphalt pavement behind a white building. Behind them, a fence hid the world. Wulf could hear traffic and smell trees and flowers beyond that fence. In front of him was a door. About fifty yards away he saw a couple of dumpsters.

The door to the white building opened and the same small man he'd seen in the warehouse waved at the guards.

"Bring them in. This way!"

The ten of them filed in. They walked slowly, encumbered by their chains, through a carpeted hall and past many rooms. Some of the doors to the rooms were opened and Wulf saw a row of washing machines, then a kitchen, then an area with tables and chairs that looked like a private dining room.

Eventually they came to a living area with sofas and chairs, and a low table in the middle. Dozens of other chained and naked humans sat on those sofas, or stood by the window looking out at an outside path and a tall hedge of oleanders.

The small man, wearing a pinstripe suit, clapped his hands. A taller man in a tuxedo with a tablet stood beside him.

"All right. Now if you haven't checked in, see Dab here with the tablet. He's got all your info. Today you will be sold to your trainers. Two trainers from the Slave Palace will be in the audience. If you do your best, you may end up there, and that is your goal, for they have the best accommodations including education if you require it, health-care and trainers who know their stuff. If you cooperate, you won't be hurt. A life of pleasure awaits you all and I know it sucks that you have no better choice, but you aren't here because you're upstanding citizens, or anything. So you could have it far worse, imprisoned for life, or living a life on the streets in abject poverty, or working the mines in the West Virgin Territories. So, there you have it. Any questions?"

Wulf could not believe it. This man was acting as if they were all going to Disneyworld.

Parcival stared directly at Wulf, then addressed his guards. "Why are you guarding him so fiercely?"

"He's trouble. He attacked us. Dewey's got a broken nose."

Parcival frowned. "Dab, come here."

Dab came over with his tablet.

"What's your name?" Parcival demanded, staring up at Wulf with his beady, black eyes.

Wulf pulled back, shaking off the guard's hands.

Parcival looked him up and down. "Nice. Nice. But—" He motioned to a guard nearby. All it took was a hand gesture and without warning the guard socked him so hard in the stomach that Wulf lost his breath.

"Now, Mr. Giant. What is your name?"

"Wulf," he managed to gasp.

Dab tapped his screen a few times. Parcival looked over his arm and they both seemed to be reading. Then Parcival's eyebrows rose.

"You're trouble. A lot of trouble. If I'd known you had been labeled a One-Night Thrall, I would've left you behind. Dab, why wasn't this brought to my attention?"

"I—sir, I hadn't gotten to this one yet."

"It was all in the files since last night."

"Yes, sir. I'm sorry, sir."

"It says here he killed two special forces agents."

"Nearly killed," Dab correctly.

"Nearly is almost the same. I'll get in trouble if I offer him as a trainable slave. So we'll go ahead and announce him as a One-Night Thrall. He's amazing-looking enough that he should still recoup my investment."

"Yes, sir."

Wulf glared at Parcival.

Parcival returned that glare with a half-smile. "You know what that means, don't you?"

Wulf gave a slight shake of his head.

"It means you have forfeited not only all your rights, but your life as well. A One-Night Thrall is considered too dangerous to train. I have the legal right to make that determination, and then when your money is earned out, take you to the euthanasia chambers in Dudley. Do you understand?"

That this man had the authority to sentence a man to death surprised Wulf.

"I don't care, devil-man!" Wulf said. "I will not make this worth anyone's while. They will demand their money back, and you will still kill me."

"All righty, then." Parcival nodded at his guard again.

Wulf received another punch. He strained to breathe through it this time.

Parcival moved closer to him until Wulf could smell the sourness of his breath.

"You are an enemy to my country. No one cares what happens to you."

Wulf forced a grin. "I know."

Parcival sneered, then stepped back and turned away.

"Gag him," Parcival ordered his guards. "I won't have him mouthing off to that fine crowd out there."

Wulf watched him clap his hands again.

Guards forced Wulf's head forward. A ball-gag was put into his mouth. It tasted of defeat.

"Now ladies and gentlemen, it's only minutes until show time. You will be stared at, you will be poked, you will be prodded, but you have no rights and no chance of escape, so as long as you remain docile, no harm will come from it. I assure you, I run a clean show. Now, are we all ready?"

No one answered.

Wulf watched as the women were put into one line, the men in another. All appeared nervous but deflated. No one cried as he had expected. He was kept apart from both.

24

It only took about fifteen minutes before all the women had been filed out and came back in to the waiting area. Then the men left. There were more of them. That line up took over twenty minutes to complete.

When it was his turn to be escorted out, Wulf did not make it easy on his guards. Why should he? He had no thing left to lose.

The guards tugged and shoved him out the door and past an alcove. A black velvet curtain hung in front of the second door and he was pushed through it.

An outdoor garden of tables, patios, ivy and flowers surrounded him. Glass tinkled, and plates with silver cutlery shined. Here, he did not hear the traffic, only the gentle chirps of birds, and the sound of a fountain on the far end, beyond the tables and beside a white concrete path.

Upper class men and women sat at the tables, and waiters and waitresses stood nearby to bring them anything they needed.

Of course. These were the wealthy buyers.

Though he'd already been sold to the broker, it was at night and in a warehouse. He'd been clothed.

Here, he felt his nakedness both inside and out. He clenched down on the ball gag in his mouth until his teeth hurt.

Wulf struggled with his guards but to no avail. They pushed him forward and he was forced to climb two steps to the center of the stage.

He didn't want to look at the people who were looking at him so he lifted his chin and tried to find a place to focus beyond the dining area, the patios and the fountain. Green lawn rose up past a footpath. A breath of fresh air.

He heard Parcival announce him. Heard him label him as dangerous. Well, he wasn't a murderer, he was a warrior. And now he was a prisoner. A slave consigned to an early death. He simply wanted to get away.

When the properly coiffed and manicured people at the tables started to get up and form a line to examine him closer, his gaze dropped. A tremble began in his knees. The grip of his guards tightened.

He tried to ignore his own humiliation, but could not stop the shame that washed over him, heating his skin.

A man sitting at the table closest to the stage looked up at him as if he were seeing a monster. But, no, that wasn't it. Wulf reassessed and decided he did not look at Wulf in disgust. No. He was rapt. His pink lips parted.

Wulf did not want to look at the man, but he was fascinating in two ways. One, he did not move to get up like the others to come examine him. And two, he had a composure about him that communicated complete and utter control. The man's dark hair shone, swept back from his face with some kind of gel.

He probably had curls, because even as slick as it was, there were telltale curves and kinks. His eyes were the softest brown hue, and his chiseled face sported a healthy tan. This man took care of himself. This man was not just spoiled and pampered, he had a reason to comport himself with dignity and purpose.

Wulf chastised himself for his thoughts. What purpose did a man in this place at this hour have but to purchase pleasure slaves? How could he think anything about this man was dignified, or in any way decent?

Now hands were all over him. They grabbed, they poked, they squeezed. They hurt.

Wulf's rage had already exploded too many times these past few days, but why should he contain himself? He had nothing.

Someone squeezed his cock. Someone pressed their palm against his balls. Hard. Harder. Pain shot through every part of him and Wulf cried out, unable to hold back.

He struggled against his chains, which pressed hard into his skin, and he pushed himself forward onto his toes. His

26

handlers weren't expecting him to lose his balance and come forward. But that was just what he did, body plunging off the low stage.

The environment around him spun.

The man at the front table jumped up just as Wulf fell, and caught him.

The fronts of Wulf's arms, manacled at the wrists, caught the man at his chest. The man stroked his hand up Wulf's bicep to his shoulder and held him.

"There now. These tiles are hard on the knees."

For a moment. A quick moment. A brief embrace. No one else seemed to notice. But Wulf felt it. The steadying clasp of arms. The warm caress. And he sensed the tremble in that firm body, a heavy pulse, a heat, a patient curiosity.

"Got your balance?" the man asked calmly.

Wulf raised his head and looked him in the eye.

The man met his gaze, unflinching.

It was Wulf who looked away first. He heard the man say, "All right then."

Strangely, the voice soothed him.

All of this happened in a matter of seconds before Wulf's guards hauled him behind the stage and back to the waiting room.

He expected some sort of punishment. A reprimand at least.

Instead, Parcival came into the room and yelled at Wulf's guards.

"If you let that happen again, you're all fired! You were warned about him. If you can't handle this job, I'll get people who can."

Wulf wanted to laugh. Or worse, scream.

Instead, he lowered his head and stared at the terracotta tile at his feet, teeth scraping at his gag, pretending he didn't exist.

Chapter Five - Locke

The auction went by too slowly for Locke's pleasure. The offerings were fairly tame. Boring, in fact. He barely paid attention as Malik ended up bidding on and winning six females of varying heights, hues and ages.

When the men returned one by one to the stage, Locke did his duty. Every male he wanted he won. Price was no object.

At last the guards brought out the One-Night Thrall. Wulf.

The man had one of those incredible physiques where the muscles, tight and toned, didn't bunch up or look like pouches of gravel, but had developed smooth and rounded, the skin like silk flowing over them. His thigh muscles were wide but long, and they tapered up to a line just below the rounded buttocks, perfectly in tune with the hips, giving his ass a heart shape.

Locke preferred a slim, straight physique, not bodies topped by huge shoulders or attached to tree-trunk thighs.

This man had the perfect physique.

His nipples were small and brown, tight little nubs drawn out by the muscle but not too much. And that proud cock and balls. Sculpted in pale gold. Intact, not cut, which Locke liked, too. It meant the head of the penis would be all the more sensitive.

Even the man's eyes, though frigid as the north wind, were fucking gorgeous. Add to that the fact that Wulf was labeled as dangerous, and Locke could not look away.

At Locke's side, Malik gave a quick laugh. "You're enamored. Quite smitten, I should think. I haven't seen that in you in years."

"I am not," Locke retorted.

"You are. You're completely enraptured by him. His behavior is quite appalling, but he is a beauty. I didn't think you were so shallow."

During training sessions of the past, Locke had had sex often. But he had not had a relationship with anyone in years, or sex in many months. His job took up all his time.

His last relationship had been with another trainer, and it had been all right at first, then completely unfulfilling. Maybe it was because he worked in the pleasure industry that most everyone had become boring to him. At least sexually. All the intellectuals he knew were merely friends.

"I'm not shallow, you ass, and I'm not enraptured. Where did you come up with that word anyway?"

"What? The word *shallow*?"

Locke smirked.

Malik leaned closer to him. "I have an idea."

"Fuck you and your ideas."

Malik said, "Oh but wait. Hear me out. You're bored. I'm bored. Day to day everything's the same, I train the slaves, they cry, they protest, they come—some quite nicely—and they go, most with a smile on their dazzled faces. But how about a challenge?"

Locke started to say no but Malik kept talking.

"I'll bet you a month's salary you can't take this One-Night Thrall and tame him."

"I don't have the time to waste."

"You would be training him on your off hours, of course. And I'll give you, say, ten days. If you don't tame him, I win the bet. And he can be sold off or put down, I don't care. But you are the best trainer at the palace. And you look like you need a challenge to put a little light back into your eyes."

"Fuck off."

"Well? Does that mean you don't want to take the bet?" Malik asked, eyes glimmering.

"You're an ass. Have I told you that?" said Locke.

"Several times already just today."

Beautiful and dangerous. Wulf was just the sort of project puzzle Locke might enjoy.

These days, everyone who came to the palace was too easy. The palace trainers and even the Eminent Masters who went to auctions like this one usually took the most beautiful and complacent untrained slaves. They guaranteed a good profit; after all, this was a business.

Locke didn't believe he was as jaded as Malik, but life at the palace was pretty routine. Every slave was a challenge, some more than others. But this one? Wulf would be interesting to say the least.

"I'd need a month minimum with him," Locke said. His heart rate increased at the simple prospect that he might take this bet.

"Are you saying you're not up to the task? Ten days is the offer on the table."

Locke did not have to consider it. This wasn't about money. For either of them. It was simply what happened when people hit their mid-thirties. They started questioning everything about their lives up to that point.

He raised a hand and scratched at his chin to hide the fact that his body was doing crazy things. Arousal, yes, perhaps somewhat. But more, a knot began to form in his stomach. Within it swirled a mixture of dread and euphoric anticipation. As if he were about to visit the dentist and embark upon a long-awaited journey at the same time.

Grinning, Malik didn't have to say another word, and he knew it.

Locke looked at him sideways and said, "Ten days."

Malik let out a huge laugh, and waved the waiter over to bring Locke a fresh bottle of wine.

Locke ignored him. He looked up at the stage again. Wulf stood there looking like a lovely, forlorn beast. But also ready to take down anyone in his way if an opening presented itself.

30

For a moment it seemed there wasn't enough air in the room. Then Locke found his voice.

"I'll bid twenty for him."

Parcival looked up from the side of the stage. "Twenty dollars? I expected to start the bidding low for a dangerous creature such as this. But the auction has not yet begun, sir— um—your Eminence."

Locke didn't want to draw this out. And besides, something about Wulf's discomfort, and the fact that they were discussing his death in front of him, was beginning to annoy him. Slaves had no rights, but prolonging the often necessary tortures they must endure when a point had already been made was overkill.

"Twenty thousand, I meant. It just saves time if I offer it up front. I don't think anyone else will challenge me."

Gasps came from behind him, drowning out the splash of the fountain.

It was more than any single slave had gone for all afternoon. He glanced about at the tables and the people behind him.

Locke didn't care if they thought he was reckless. Or even crazy. It was less than half of what he made in a month. He wouldn't be using the Palace's money. So who should care what he did?

"You understand that this man is not an investment on any future. You cannot get your investment back on a One-Night Thrall."

"I am in Eminent Master of the Slave Palace. Of course I understand," he snapped.

Parcival bowed his head and stepped back. "Done," was all he said.

Chapter Six - Wulf

Wulf could not believe the stern handsome buyer at the front table purchased him for a near fortune. This was the same man who had kept him from falling off the stage less than an hour ago. A man who gripped him a little longer than he needed to after Wulf regained his balance. Not that he cared. He would be dead in a day or two anyway.

But he could not help but wonder. Why this man? Why had he paid so much money for a slave that could not return the investment?

Wulf knew he had a great body, a warrior's body, but if that were the extent of it, why not allow the auction to begin and get him for a lower cash amount?

When his guards escorted him back to the waiting room, he was shoved in the line up of slaves destined for the Slave Palace.

But that couldn't be right. As everyone in the world knew, the Slave Palace had a reputation for training and dealing in the best bred, strongest, most beautiful and complacent humans. Wulf was missing one of those components. He was anything but complacent. He'd been marked a dangerous.

The Slave Palace would never risk bringing him into their sanctum.

Yet the computers were checked. Doubled checked. He was stamped on the wrist and given a new neck band. His ball-gag was removed.

The guard holding Wulf's gag glared at him. "No more mouthing off or this goes back in place, understand?"

Wulf swallowed the built-up saliva in his mouth, and nodded.

The slaves in Wulf's line were also allowed lightweight shoes, but no clothing. Each one was given a clean white towel and instructed to use it folded under their buttocks for sitting.

Wulf boarded the Slave Palace bus outside the back doors where the fence blocked the city traffic. Again and again he read the words emblazoned on the side of the vehicle.

Slave Palace Transport.

He was going to the Slave Palace. It had to be a mistake. They didn't deal in slaves who'd been labeled as he had been. But no one stopped him.

Of course he didn't want to go to the Slave Palace, or any slave quarters in existence. He wanted to die. But it might have been worse. At least the man who bought him didn't look like some sleazy sadist.

Wulf kept his mouth shut and boarded the bus. It was difficult with the manacles and chains, but he managed. He put his neatly folded towel on the seat beside a smaller male with spiked white hair, and sat.

The man turned to him, leaning away. "You're the One-Night Thrall."

Wulf did not reply.

Immediately submissive, the man said, "I'm sorry. There's nowhere else to sit or I'd give you the whole seat."

Wulf noticed the man was actually shaking. Wulf closed his eyes and pretended not to see him.

He heard the man sigh and felt the seat jerk as he leaned back. This man was afraid of him. Somehow, that made Wulf feel better.

Wulf kept looking at the clock on the driver's dashboard. He had not seen a clock in days. He didn't even know the date.

The trip ended after less than twenty minutes.

Right now it was four twenty-one p.m.

The Slave Palace loomed before him.

It looked like something out of a fairy tale with battlements between looming towers topped with pointed gold turrets. There was a guard wall and a heavy gate made of iron bars thick as Wulf's arm.

Wulf tried to see beyond the gate, but too many uniformed guards stood in the way.

After a brief stop at the gate, it swung open for the van, which drove up a fancy tiled drive lined with rocks, grass, and large oaks.

Beautiful statues of naked men and women posed like gods on pedestals scattered across the lawns. More statues appeared closer together where the drive curved toward wide steps that led to two red double doors about twelve feet tall.

Wulf was the first to disembark, moving slowly down the steps of the van, his chains stretched tight. It was hard not to fall. His hands were chained to his waist and were no help for his balance. In one of his hands, he held his towel.

When he stood on firm ground, four guards immediately surrounded him. He ignored them, glancing about.

The nearest statue, a beautiful bluish marble carving of a nude young man with one arm raised behind his head, caught Wulf's attention. Magnificent in detail, Wulf had the urge to examine it closer—until it moved.

It wasn't a sculpture at all. As he stared at it, he realized it was a real man painted in smooth, blue-speckled liquid that made his skin and hair look like marble. The shift in his pose had been slight, but Wulf had caught it. As he stared, he could see the man's flat, hairless chest rise and fall with each breath he took.

Wulf turned his head to look beyond the van and across the drive to the other statues scattered about, some as far away as the outer walls, and realized they were all people, real people. The men and women were painted to look like white, blue or green marble. Some looked like weathered metal. All of them were living beings.

"What's the matter, giant? Never seen a statue before?" asked one guard.

The others all chuckled.

"Hey!"

Wulf looked up at the new voice as all the other slaves from the van gathered behind him.

The double doors to the palace were open. A young man with short brown hair stood on the threshold wearing a white suit with tails. Underneath the jacket he had on a white vest and a shirt with the collar buttoned all the way to his neck. His hands clasped behind his back.

"New slaves are to be treated with utmost respect," he said as if addressing the air.

The guards stood straighter, all amusement gone from their faces.

"Now," said the man in the doorway. He looked down at the group flanking Wulf. "I would like to welcome you all to the Slave Palace. Do not be afraid. As long as you obey your masters and do everything you are told, you will know only luxury and pleasure for the rest of your lives. You have been chosen among many for this special privilege. For people such as yourselves, who have lost all inalienable rights to freedom for varying reasons, you could not have hoped for a better outcome than standing here among us right now. For this is a new era in your life, and if you embrace it well, it can bring you external benefit and internal peace the likes of which you have only dreamed. Some of you are criminals; some of you are prisoners of war. You have made past mistakes that cannot be righted, but none of you will be responsible for bad decisions ever again. Your every act will be dictated by your masters. You need not think any further than your master's orders and will."

He stopped, eyes passing over the crowd and stopping at Wulf.

Wulf scowled.

"I can see some of you are afraid and trembling. Or angry and in denial. But I will tell you all, this is quite a freeing process. To learn how to be a slave, to give pleasure on command, or to receive it on command, is not a punishment, it is a reward. You are the lucky ones being rewarded today. Perhaps none of you feel you deserve this, but you are here now and the deal is done.

"Never forget as you enter this grand establishment. You are now a commodity this country values the most, to be treasured, revered and trained.

"And so, without further delay, I welcome you."

Wulf rolled his eyes. What an act. The man seemed to think they should be grateful to be here. Chained. Naked. The former existence of each one of them wiped into nothingness.

He moved forward with the others, ascending the front steps and entering a great, airy hall.

The floor was tiled white with blue patterns of fleur-de-lis. A sloping ramp led down to the main landing. Surrounding them, grand golden pillars rose every ten feet, holding up a second story balcony on either side of the huge room.

Wulf saw people walking and standing on those balconies. Some turned to look their way as they entered. Only about half of them appeared to be clothed.

The area was so huge it reminded Wulf of a mall. In fact, that's exactly what it was, with staircases at each end in each corner leading up to the second level. And on both levels there were closed doors leading to unknown rooms.

The ceiling stretched up and up to a high tower made of glass. It let the light in and it came down in shafts of pinks, blues, purples and golds.

Ornate wrought-iron railings with curlicues and leaf designs decorated the open, upper level. The frames around each door were thick wood carved with images of naked men and women flowing into each other. The walls were painted deep red, and every space held a work of framed art of humans in erotic poses, or groups of humans in erotic tangles.

It was too much to take in all at once.

Wulf felt like he'd gone from the twenty-first century back in time to some over-dramatic, ostentatious castle of a despot king.

Everything was about sex and pleasure. Decadence. Vice. Moral decay.

Here he stood, naked in the midst of all of it. Caught in the currents of Avilan's evil, an evil he'd spent five years — most of his adult life since he'd turned eighteen — fighting against. And lost.

He'd failed everything and everyone he'd ever known. He was not fit to live.

It made him a bit more content to remember he would not be here for long in this decadent castle, or on this Earth. For he was to be put down. Parcival's handlers had made sure he knew it.

After a minute of gawking at their surroundings, the group of slaves was approached by several formal-looking men and women dressed in black slacks and black, long-sleeved shirts. They wore thick leather belts, boots and gloves. On their belts hung arrays of tools. Sex tools, Wulf noted. There were whips of varying sizes, chains, handcuffs, and rows of vials that could be medicine or perfume or lubricating oils.

Slowly, these trainers came forward and separated the new slaves into groups. Men in one group, women in another.

One man came toward Wulf. For a moment, Wulf thought he was the man who'd bid on him in the garden auction. But no, this man was younger and far sharper-featured, with a hard gaze.

"Come with me please." The man's voice held no inflection. No emotion.

With a quick snap, he fastened a leash to Wulf's collar and led him away from the group.

On instinct, Wulf pulled back against the chain the man now held. The man jerked it hard, and a sharp shock went through Wulf's body from his neck to his toes. The pain came hard and fast. His cock throbbed painfully. His balls stung.

The shock was gone as quickly as it came, but it had completely incapacitated him for a second. He was surprised he did not pass out.

Calmly, the man said, "That was not even a mid-level setting. I will not ask again."

Wulf frowned in disbelief, then followed him beyond the large hall to a set of double doors.

They walked down more lavish corridors, these painted white with sconces that looked old-fashioned and made blue shadows upon the walls.

Finally, the man leading Wulf turned into a room. It looked like an office.

The man led Wulf to a hook in the wall and attached his leash to it. Wulf dared not pull against it for fear of a repeat of that terrible shock.

The man, content with where he'd left Wulf, took his towel from hi and threw it into a hamper. He then went to a black desk and turned on a computer. He sat, took off his leather gloves, and typed on the keyboard, making little huffing noises under his breath.

After a couple of minutes, he got up with a tablet in one hand, and with the other took something from his belt.

Wulf could not see what was in his hand until he held it up, and then he almost sighed in relief. The man held a tape measure. He used it painstakingly to measure every inch of Wulf's body from neck to ankles, including measuring the length and girth of his flaccid cock. He made notes on the tablet as he went.

Next, he put on a pair of rubber gloves and walked behind Wulf, touching him on the buttocks.

Wulf said, "No."

The man said, "Do not move, please."

"*Please*?" Wulf snorted. "Are you asking my permission?"

"No. I'm simply being polite." The man still had no inflection in his tone. "If it helps you, I am a doctor."

"It doesn't." But strangely, Wulf's body relaxed at the knowledge. As if some inner program inside his physical body told him this was acceptable when clearly he had not consented.

The man pulled Wulf's buttocks apart.

Without thinking, Wulf jerked against his chain. The shock went through him like a sword going from the roof of his mouth all the way through his gullet and coming out at the groin. His legs trembled.

An echo of a low scream still reverberated in the room. Wulf realized seconds later it had been his own voice.

Tears stung his cheeks.

Still chained at the waist, his hands could not move to wipe them away.

The doctor stood, hands off, and watched him.

Wulf did not cringe under the stare, but inside he wanted to curl into a ball and die already.

The doctor said, "That was a much higher setting that time. Now. Shall we try this again? Stand still. Please."

Wulf gritted his teeth.

Hands parted his buttocks. Something cold touched his most intimate of places. The tip of a finger entered, then was gone.

That entry into his body was almost as much of a shock to him as the collar. His muscles froze, not in pain but humiliation. But, he told himself, why should he be humiliated? His body was no longer his. And at the auction, the potential buyers had done far worse to him in their examinations.

The doctor took off the gloves and put on more. He examined Wulf's ears, eyes and the inside of his mouth. He made more notes.

He went back to his computer and typed again. Wulf did not want to be caught staring at him, so he turned away but kept the man in his peripheral vision.

Now the man got up and went to a cabinet behind the desk. He took out two syringes. Both looked silver and huge. He came over the Wulf and stood in front of him.

He held up the first syringe. "This one is a combo of vitamins and an immunity booster. You are not from our country. You may be exposed to things your body isn't normally used to."

He held up the second syringe. "This one holds a microchip. It will be placed under your skin so should you ever become lost, we can find you."

"Lost?" Wulf asked. "Really?"

The doctor did not reply. He held the first silver syringe to Wulf's upper arm and there was a click. Wulf felt only a brief sting like air, no needle. The doctor then walked behind Wulf and scooped up his hair, pushing it to the side. The second syringe felt cold against the back of his neck. It made a loud thunk instead of a click. The sting became a burning sensation that radiated outward, slow to recede.

The hand let go of his hair. "There," said the implacable voice. "All done."

The doctor went back to his desk. He typed for a few more seconds, then picked up his cell.

"Yes," he said into the phone. "He's ready."

A knock came at the door and it opened.

A female all in black entered. She went to the wall where Wulf's leash was attached and unhooked the clasp. Unlike the doctor, she smiled at him sweetly when she said, "Come along."

Wulf followed her into the corridor.

"This way," she said. "No tugging. You know what happens if you pull on the leash."

Wulf did not respond.

"I'm told your name is Wulf. I like that. You are quite a specimen. You're lucky to be here. Normally the masters don't purchase slaves who are uncontrollable."

"You mean dangerous?" Wulf asked.

"I wouldn't say that. But yes, you did successfully attack and injure two very highly-trained professional combat soldiers. That is their point of view, of course. Yours could be that you were defending yourself."

Wulf swallowed hard. She talked fast. As if this was normal. But it was normal for her. This was her job day in, day out.

"Anyway, there must be some reason Eminent Master Locke purchased you."

"Eminent Master?" Now Wulf had a name to put to the face of the man who bought him. *Locke.*

"Oh yes. He's one of the highest ranking masters of the Slave Palace. And one of the youngest to ever claim a seat on the Board. He bought you as a personal slave, not to be trained with the others. To my knowledge, he's never ever done that before. Well, I'm helping him as a favor. There was no one else available to take you to your quarters."

"You mean cell," Wulf interjected.

"No. Your quarters. Anyway, Master Locke's been so good to me. I've only worked here two years and I've already gotten three raises. Just last week, he gave me another raise."

Wulf wondered what she did to deserve such raises. Did she beat the slaves just a bit harder than the other trainers? Did she make them suffer sexually?

It was funny to look at her with her young eyes and innocent complexion. She didn't seem the type.

"I'm Bunny, by the way," she said. She kept talking as they walked, careful to keep Wulf's leash low in her hand, sagging.

"You're quite a looker. Very nice. Maybe that's what caught Master Locke's attention. But then, I don't know. He's around beauty every day, all day. After awhile, you see beyond that. I wonder what he saw in you? More than danger. More than a big cock."

Three days ago, Wulf would have been appalled at her statement. Now, he barely acknowledged it.

"Master Locke wouldn't risk bringing danger into the Palace unless he had good reason," she went on. "So what is it?"

She kept turning her head, looking him up and down. Wulf hated the scrutiny.

"Was Doctor Torvalis totally horrid?" She gave a small laugh. "He's so funny. He barely talks. Grunts. Some of the people around here call him Doctor Grunt. He takes his job here waaaay too seriously. But he is the best. Or so they say here at the Palace."

She made two turns down two long halls. Finally, she stopped, took a key from her busy belt, and unlocked the door.

"Here we are," she said and stepped past the threshold.

Wulf had no choice but to follow, keeping his leash slack.

He almost gasped to see the room. "Is this Master Locke's room?"

"No, silly. Yours."

"But I'm a prisoner."

"Well, maybe, in a way. But the bars of this prison aren't metal. Well, maybe they are out front, but not in here."

"This is my cell?"

She laughed. "Yes. It is. You're lucky to have it to yourself. All new slaves share with a roommate. But Master Locke put you here by yourself. Maybe because you're *dangerous*." She said the last word with sarcasm, as if this were all some joke.

Wulf looked around. The bed was huge, draped with a gray-blue comforter and stacked with upright pillows at the headboard: blue, green, gray. At the foot of the bed were two reclining chairs upholstered in gray and white. They faced a long window that took up the entire length of the wall.

In front of the window was a white ledge scattered with green and blue pillows. The view looked out over a sweeping lawn. From here, Wulf could see the palace battlements, and beyond them—for the palace was on a softly sloping hill—the endless buildings and towers of a city. Lirangel, it was called. The capital of Avilan.

Another joke of cruelty, this was, for giving a slave such a view only cemented the knowledge into them that they would never be free to go into such a world except or unless they were sold.

For Wulf, the cruelty ran deeper. For he was slated to die.

"Isn't it beautiful?" Bunny asked.

Wulf turned away. Past the bed to the left were two more softly padded arm-chairs facing a white fireplace with a black grate. Everything smelled clean, like lemons. Above the fireplace, fresh flower blooms of yellow and orange spilled over the edged of an expensive-looking green vase. The fireplace was flanked by two floor-to-ceiling mirrors, giving the room an even more spacious feel.

Bunny motioned to the open doorway in the wall at the left of the room's entrance.

"This is the bathroom."

She turned back to face him.

"You are allowed to take your shoes off here, and put them on when you leave, but otherwise it is against the rules to wear any clothing. You should also know that your collar is not to be removed at any time. To do so will result in more shocks. You also cannot leave this room without an official escort, such as me, the doctor, or your master. If you try to leave this space on your own, the room's security system will activate the collar. The system automatically comes on as soon as I leave. Sorry, that's just the way it is."

Wulf stood staring out the long window. He thought it must be almost five o'clock by now. Autumn. The sun was already starting to set. The sea of lights from the city were already coming on. Wouldn't the statues be cold?

Out the corner of his eye, Wulf saw Bunny turn and put her hand on the door. Just before she left, she muttered, "I wish I knew why Eminent Master Locke purchased you."

The door closed.

Wulf wished he knew why as well.

Chapter Seven – Locke

Locke sat back in his recliner and watched the large flat screen in his private suite.

The cameras were hidden in every part of Wulf's room, including the bathroom and shower. For new slaves, it was necessary to keep an eye on them every minute. The collars could only do so much to curb some behaviors.

Occasionally, new slaves, despite intense vetting, tried to destroy palace property. Some tried to hurt or even kill themselves.

Wulf did not try to do any of those things. Instead, he moved about the room, panther-like, examining every surface floor to ceiling, even under the bed.

The way his body flexed, arched, walked, sat or stood exuded a gracefulness that proved great discipline and training. Wulf was a very talented and capable creature. Locke could see that in these first few minutes of viewing him. It was why he'd taken Malik's bet in the first place and bought the man.

There was nothing different, strange or wrong about Wulf. Simply, he'd been born in another country, a country that, unfortunately, had decided Avilan was their enemy. And that put Wulf in predatory mode. As a predator, he was magnificent.

The fact that Wulf considered everyone around him an enemy was a challenge for Locke. People like Wulf saw things in blacks and whites, no shades of gray.

If Locke were going to win his bet, he would have to get Wulf to consider all the shades of the color palette of life. Considering the fact that Wulf was no longer free didn't matter. People who were close to meeting their fates could learn new lessons quite quickly. Especially lessons of the heart and soul.

Not that Locke had any intention of putting him down. Unless things got completely out of hand. But Wulf didn't know that yet.

Every move Wulf made fed like art into Locke's brain. Little thrills of pleasure zinged all over his body. And when Wulf finished examining the room and approached the fresh flowers, leaning in to smell them, Locke's skin warmed on his arms, hips, legs. His cock shifted.

Locke had great control of himself. He became aroused when he wanted to. When he allowed himself to. This — this was different. New.

Malik had used the word *enraptured*. Of course Locke knew the meaning, but later he'd looked up the word online. One of the definitions was *intoxicated*. It fit. Like the finest of wines, Wulf had crossed his path.

Another definition of the word was *captivated*. Captivated. He could not get that word out of his head. Because if Locke really was enraptured, it implied that Locke might be just as much a captive, in a way, as Wulf was.

The idea of that made Locke's balls tingle. The fever on his skin increased.

He'd been working too hard. That was it.

He hummed low in his throat.

All this was new and different for him. New because he never bought slaves for training that weren't already subservient, their situations and crimes always of the non-violent sort. It was the policy of the Slave Palace, and his own agenda as well. A violent mind could not be trusted unless a lot of psychological work was done beforehand. The Slave Palace was not in the practice of reforming violent criminals. Nor was it in the business of selling One-Night Thralls.

But Wulf was Locke's purchase. A personal bet. And yes, he could not deny his instant infatuation. And so he'd bought a One-Night Thrall. And now the game became of interest.

How to train him? How to tame him?

Another question came to him. Was Wulf actually a violent criminal by definition? An enemy to the state, yes. But war made ordinary men into killers. They even perceived themselves as heroes. Whether they were or not was beside the point. Wulf might hate the country of Avilan, and serve willingly in a military that raised him to fight, but that did not mean he wanted to murder each and every citizen in their sleep.

This was something Locke might be able to work with. If, that was, Wulf even wanted to live.

It had been a long time since Locke had taken a slave in hand and trained him (or her) from the ground up. Since he'd garnered a seat on the Slave Palace board and become an Eminent Master, he'd overseen final training exercises, given orders, and critically fine-tuned methods and strategies, but it had been a cold performance only. He also watched final graduation performances, wrote up his reports, gave his thumbs up or thumbs down. He didn't have time for anything else.

Malik still trained slaves, skin to skin, from the bottom up. He enjoyed his work. He enjoyed all the pleasures and commented often about it. He told Locke he never wanted to do anything else.

When Locke had taken his seat on the board, Malik had said, "You're too young for that."

For Malik, the added paperwork would have kept him from the pleasures he loved. He'd declined an offer to the Board so he could stay closer to the slaves' daily lives.

But Locke had been ready. The slave training was fun but left him hollow. He excelled at it, or he would not have gained his title so early in his life, but administrative duties gave him another sense of power, for he oversaw and controlled the daily dealings of all the slaves in training, and made decisions on everything from how they presented themselves, to how much each should be priced. He was able to deny customers at the flick of a cursor. He could make slaves repeat their training if they needed it, or introduce them to stronger methods.

Any complaints or problems within the palace that landed on his desk were his to oversee. He made decisions that fixed or eradicated any drama. No day was boring.

It was a heady feeling.

It made him revered, and both loved and hated.

Now he watched as Wulf slowed his prowl about the room. Finally, the man sat on the edge of the bed.

From Wulf's file, Locke read he'd come straight from the military prison where he'd refused food. He had then been put on a plane and taken to another holding cell, only to be sold a day later to the slave broker, Parcival.

Wulf had to be tired. No doubt, he'd barely had time to assess his situation. He probably had not slept much. And if he'd refused meals, Locke had to wonder when the last time he ate was.

First things first. What does one do with a feral animal they want to tame?

Offer it food, of course.

*

Locke placed his thumb on the door's security system. Recognizing his print, it unlocked.

A pretty young slave named Sky, who was repeating his manners lessons, attended. Sky stood naked and lithe at Locke's side holding a covered tray containing a sumptuous meal of rib eye, baked potato, green beans and peach pie. The scent of the steak still sizzling in its juices would make anyone not a vegetarian salivate.

Wulf's files did not indicate he was a vegetarian. But this meal would allow Locke to learn at least that much about him.

He opened the door.

Wulf sat on the edge of his bed. His head jerked up as Locke entered, the slave trailing behind him.

Watching Wulf on the cameras for the last couple of hours did little to communicate Wulf's true magnificence. Seeing him again in person, Locke had to force himself to remember to breathe.

Was it just he who was affected by this man's immediate virility and ability to fill the room with his aura?

Locke glanced at Sky to see if the younger slave had any reaction, but Sky, dutiful and obedient, and determined to pass his manners test by the end of the month, kept his gaze on the tray in his hand.

Willing the tingle of arousal away, Locke stepped forward.

"Sky, please put the tray on the table by the left gray chair."

Wulf did not stand at Locke's presence. A problem, but expected. And minor compared to everything else Locke knew he faced with this one.

Despite everything that had happened to Wulf in the past few days—fighting, defeat, captivity, being sold at auction as a thrall only to be put to death—Wulf lifted his chin in a show of strength. Maybe even defiance.

And that laced Locke's blood with a heated thrill.

His very own slave again, his to train, and such a superb specimen.

When Sky put the tray down, Locke turned to him. "You may go."

"Yes, Eminent Master." Sky bowed gracefully—he was learning well—and exited the room.

"The meal is for you," Locke began. "The rib eye is rare, the way I take it. I am assuming you are hungry and tired. So your training begins with this, a simple meal."

Wulf did not move. He watched Locke with a wary gaze, shoulders back, his palms at rest on the tops of his thighs.

Locke blinked slowly, meeting that gaze with his own strength of will.

"You should understand that this situation is uncommon. The good news is you are to be trained. You will not be killed immediately as your broker intended."

Locke decided to come clean with the truth immediately. He wanted Wulf to feel somewhat safe, but still feel the anvil of his mortality hanging over his head.

"You are labeled as dangerous, but I see from your records that your aggressions have so far been in battle, which includes a perfectly reasonable reaction to fight your captors."

"Is not everything a battle?" Wulf asked.

Locke's body tingled. The voice was as beautiful as the man.

Locke lifted an eyebrow. "Indeed. The struggle to survive."

Wulf did not reply.

Locke said, "That struggle includes keeping oneself fed and healthy. Right now, you need to eat."

Wulf glanced at the tray on the table between the two lounge chairs that faced the view of the city lights. His throat muscles moved as Wulf seemingly could not control his need to swallow.

"And if I take my steak well-done?" Wulf asked.

"You are not in a position to make that decision."

At Locke's statement, the muscles of Wulf's face hardened along the jaw line and cheekbones. He was clenching his teeth.

Wulf met Locke's eyes. "You're the one from the garden auction."

50

"Yes."

"When I fell—"

"Yes."

"It is interesting that you think you are doing me any favors at all."

"It is interesting that you think my actions are favors," Locke replied.

"You are preserving my life. You call that good news?"

Locke frowned. "At the point where you were sold to the broker, whether your life was forfeit or preserved was not your decision to make. When I bought you, it was my decision to stay your execution. For me, that is good news. Otherwise, what a waste of your—uh—attributes." He smiled with that final word.

"Your decision? Do I not belong to the Slave Palace now?"

"No. But even if you did, I make such decisions and assessments daily for Palace slaves."

"Then if I don't belong to the Palace, why am I here?"

"Because," said Locke, "you belong to me now."

Wulf's eyebrows rose. "You?"

Locke turned away. "Enough questions for now."

"Why?"

Locke ignored Wulf and went to the lounge chair. He sat and folded his hands across his abdomen. He waited.

"Why?" Wulf asked again.

"You will eat now," Locke said. "It is a very small thing I ask. And for your own health and well-being."

Silence followed.

Locke waited without a word, without moving a muscle.

The hotplate kept the steak sizzling, its fire-seared odor permeating the air. Locke had already eaten, but even full, his saliva glands responded.

This had to be torture for Wulf.

Long ago, at the inception of this job, Locke had learned infinite patience. Training was, strangely, a form of meditation. For both trainer and trainee. To become an Eminent Master, he had learned the art of discipline, both for body and mind.

Controlling the slave through the electrical device on their collar was easy. Controlling their emotional response to their situation was the hard part. First, a trainer needed impeccability of self. Becoming enraged, yelling, screaming, violence... that was never a way to treat or teach anyone, including a slave.

Locke stared at the whip hanging off the side of his belt. A tool. Meant mostly to intimidate, to discipline, but never in anger. Never in violent outbursts. The best masters did not need to resort to any harm, and Locke rarely used such tools. Training was an art. If treated as an art form, the slave responded in kind.

Locke forced himself to remain in the chair. Unmoving. Silent. He gazed out the long window past the Palace battlements at the view of Lirangel, its confetti of lights: soft blue, gold, blinking red.

The towers of the city were jagged silhouettes dappled with white luminescence. The new evening sky was a deep purple. From this distance, nothing about the city was garish, concrete, or cold, as most cities were. For the moment, it seemed a fairytale sight from where the great Palace on the hill overlooked it.

Locke had seen the Palace from a distant vantage first as a child. It had a holiday spangle to it year-round.

But what might Wulf, who had never grown up here, see? An alien world, Locke thought. Sinful, of course, as Rille was a country that prided itself on the belief that pleasure equaled shame, especially sexual pleasure. The country's courting rituals involved chaperones, and marriages were arranged. Wulf also probably thought Lirangel was dangerous, full of crime lords who traded in human flesh, and slave brokers who sold people like Wulf to be raped and killed. Of course, that was true, but not the norm.

Locke wondered what it might be like to be raised in a culture where pleasure was seen as a sin. He had never felt ashamed of his body, or the bodies of others. Not once. The body was an art form. To be deprived of such art, that was the sin, the crime.

Locke had ten days to convince Wulf to his side. To tame him.

Of course, he had longer. He owned Wulf now. His bet with Malik was merely a dalliance. But still, the ten day deadline gave him a thrill. Could he do it? The funny thing was, few could tame a feral kitten in ten days. And Wulf was no kitten.

He waited. He refused to look at his watch. The time seemed to stretch. He would wait for hours if he had to.

Locke affixed his gaze on one blinking light far out on the sea of colorful city-stars, and sent his mind into a meditative doze.

The soft crush of footfalls on carpet roused Locke. He blinked.

He did not know how much time had passed, but the night looked deeper, and the city seemed almost sleepy.

Locke kept very still as he saw movement in his peripheral vision. A naked, beautiful man came to stand before the view, but he wasn't looking outward. He was gazing at the table. At the tray of food still fresh on its warming plate.

More waiting.

Wulf swallowed, an audible gulp. Locke's heart skipped. He could see the lovely profile, the pale hair with stripes of deep gold sweeping in tangles at the shoulders. Straight of form, Wulf stood as if he'd been trained to look that good, shoulders back, hips straight, hands at his sides with the fingers slightly curled, stomach clenched, fit, tight.

So pleasant to see even if Locke pretended not to look.

Finally, Wulf bent and reached for the tray. He took it up, holding it as if to sniff the fragrances of the meal.

There was really nowhere to take the tray, set it, and sit down to eat. Locke realized this a moment too late. Normally, all slaves ate in the community cafeterias and dining halls. A dining table was not normal fare in the quarters, even lavish quarters such as this suite.

Finally, seeing no other way, Wulf sat, tray in hand, body gracefully bending to the chair. He set the tray on his bare thighs. The balance of it seemed to be a problem, and Locke realized it was because he was shaking.

Despite stimulants and vitamin shots, the man was starving.

Wulf managed. Barely. He took the cover off the plate, picked up the steak with his bare hands and bit into it. Grease rolled down his fingers to his wrists. He hardly chewed, he was so ravenous. He tore into the meat, which parted like butter at each bite, and in about a minute, the steak was gone.

Locke turned to him, then. He spoke with affected nonchalance.

"In the slave halls, you would be punished for that."

Wulf looked at him, steak juices glimmering on his lips, which he flattened in a rude, ugly look. Then with his glistening fingers, he picked up the baked potato dripping with butter and sour cream, and bit into one end.

"Perhaps you never used utensils in Rille?" Locke said quietly.

"Perhaps a plastic knife and fork are useless on a steak," Wulf said with his mouth full.

Locke leaned forward to see the plate. Indeed, the cutlery was plastic. He'd forgotten that Wulf was labeled dangerous. No one in the Palace would give him an actual knife or fork.

Wulf continued to eat with his fingers, licking them as he went. The act might be titillating if he knew how to do it right. Instead, he was a lost child pushing food into his gullet to stave off starvation.

"How long since you had an actual meal?" Locke asked.

"I don't know." Now Wulf's mouth was filled with green beans.

Locke took a deep breath, then let it out slowly. If Wulf could not remember, then it had been too long.

When it came to the peach pie, at least Wulf wiped his greasy hands first before picking it up and taking the slice almost whole into his mouth. Locke watched the blue eyes glaze over when the meal was done.

A full belly would do that to anyone, even the most seasoned enemy soldier.

Wulf leaned back in the chair, the tray still balanced on his thighs. His stomach rose and fell with each inhale and exhale. Taut. Flat. The navel like a half-moon in a golden sky. His pecs twitched once. He closed his eyes, leaning his head on the back of the chair, blond hair falling over the edge.

Clearly, he was exhausted.

Locke could not help the wave of affection that rose over him. What was this? The man was still a stranger, and a surly one at that. *Dangerous.*

Eyes still closed, Wulf said, low, "I think I might throw up."

When one was starving and ate too fast, it happened.

Wulf did not move.

Locke said, getting up from his chair, "You may rest for the evening. You have everything you need. And if you are sick, housekeeping would appreciate it if you vomited in the toilet."

Wulf gave a groan.

Locke approached him.

Wulf jerked back, the tray on his thighs rattling when he saw Locke standing in front of him, inches away from his knees.

Calmly, Locke reached down and picked up the tray. "Now, now," he said softly.

Wulf said, "Do not touch me!"

"Oh?" Locke replied, holding the tray at waist level. "You think you have any say in what is done with you, with your body, or how, or when, or with what?"

Wulf glared.

"Now that we are finished, you may rest." Locked turned toward the door.

"That's it?"

"That's what?" Locke asked, turning his head to look at the magnificent man still sitting in the chair.

"You bring food. I eat it. That's it?"

"For this evening, yes," Locke replied.

Wulf's brows lowered. "You were here simply to watch me eat?"

"Hmm. Yes."

"Why?"

"To see how long it would take you to decide to live."

"What? You told me yourself you have the power of life and death over me!" Wulf nearly shouted.

"I could force nutrients into your system medically, I suppose," Locke said. "But that's not really living."

Wulf let out a rude, huffing sound. "So when do we begin my training in sin? In the morning?"

Locke turned all the way around, tray in hand. "My dear, we've already started."

Chapter Eight – Wulf

Things were not going as Wulf expected. The luxury of the Palace. The perfunctory attitude of the doctor. The casual, party-girl tone of Bunny. The calmness of his owner, Locke. And the food. Such quality of food as he had not had in years!

Wulf looked around his room. His *cell*. He'd never known such richness. Such finery. Satin comforters and pillows. Silk bed ruffles. Curtains like velvet. Chairs that cushioned his bottom like clouds.

He kept having to remind himself from one minute to the next that this was still a prison. He would never be free again.

And his new owner! He could barely allow himself to think of him. But how could he stop?

Locke. That was his name. He seemed harmless. Almost. His presence filled a room when he entered. It was nothing he overtly did. But a bearing he had, the way he stood, walked, spoke. All with an inner calm as if he owned the world and could decide who to present it to, and when.

Wulf had known men like this. They were important people, princes, commanders, teachers. But all of those men, and a few women, had been harshly formidable and cold, never quiet. They shouted and yelled orders. They were zealous in their agendas. But that was what one met when they joined the army at eighteen.

Wulf was twenty-three now. But he never pretended he knew anything. He was a baby compared to the leaders of men, the captains against sin, those superiors who would purge the devils of the world.

Locke was not like them at all. Locke, in his inimitable, relaxed manner was worse. He appeared to have no real agenda other than controlling Wulf. But he commanded the very air about him with his soft, low voice, his graceful manner, and the lit-up beauty that made his dark eyes and hair glow.

Locke didn't have to yell. Locke was a master. An Eminent Master, according to Bunny.

What did that mean?

It meant there would be punishment, of course. Discipline. And sex violations. That was what Wulf had been taught. That was what he knew. It was worse than any commander, captain, teacher or superior Wulf had ever known. For to be a master of pleasure slaves, this man had to be a sexual sadist. Wulf's mind could offer no other conclusion.

Why, then, did his body react to the man? With strange heat and tingling? With accelerated heart rate? More than fear or death-anxiety, this was different. Startling in its intensity. It made his stomach tie up in a knot not of pain, but strange delight. A delight that had been beaten out of him by his father when he'd hit puberty and got caught touching himself.

He hadn't known, then, the evils of such deeds. But his father taught him. His father beat him. And he never did it again.

But now? Locke caused those feelings to return. It wasn't as if he didn't have such feelings in his adult years, but he clamped down on them hard. He ignored them. He drank alcohol with his fellow warriors in his unit, pretending not to care when they secretly went into shadows with "loose" women, pretending that he was waiting for his arranged marriage to lose his virginity when really he didn't feel anything like that for women at all but might, deep down, have preferred a male. That, even more than sneaking away with women, was highly forbidden, a crime one would be put in prison for. He had thought something was wrong with him.

But all those feelings were purged from him with hard work and dedication to wiping out the forces of evil in the world that took away people's wills that allowed sexual debauchery free reign.

58

Avilan was the enemy. Avilan should not exist.

He told himself his feelings of arousal were because of the Palace itself. As he'd been escorted through the main landing, and the halls, he'd seen the erotic paintings, murals, and carvings. Scenes of all sorts depicting men with women, women with women, and most surprising, men with men. He'd tried not to look. But he must have seen with more than just a quickly averted gaze. He must already be suffering from the beginnings of brainwashing, he told himself.

He refused to become aroused. He wouldn't!

But Locke, with his tranquil smile and smooth, untroubled features continued to haunt his mind.

Locke would be back in the morning. But he'd said his lessons had already started.

Wulf's hands made fists as he got up from the chair and started to pace.

The walking helped stretch his muscles and get his digestion going. He no longer felt the need to vomit. But he was still greatly upset. Of course! Who wouldn't be? he told himself. Forced into pleasure slavery, even if Locke told the truth and he was not to be killed, he faced a lifetime of being raped and abused by his captors! By sinners! By the very devils who thought they could rule the world with their evil ways.

So many thoughts passed through him as he paced. Could he cooperate, earn trust, and then escape? Should he just get it over with and kill himself now if he could find the means? Maybe the collar, if he tugged on it enough, would deliver such a shock as to stop his heart.

But when he thought of that pain, and how it froze him in every way, he could not begin to consider that course of action.

He paced for about a half an hour before exhaustion over-took him.

He went to the bathroom and used the facilities. They had provided him with everything. Toothbrush. Comb.

Electric shaver. Washcloths, towels, soaps, and shampoos. He used them all, feeling clean and relatively human again, and made his way to the bed.

Wulf could not recall the last good night's sleep he'd had. In his unit, they had cots with lumpy, thin mattresses. In the military prison, and the cage on the airplane, he'd had only uncomfortable moments of sleep. The bed looked like a dream. His current dream. To escape into sleep. For one night, at least. He could curl into himself for warmth and comfort and let his exhaustion ride over him and turn to solace for a weary prisoner of war.

The collar chafed just a bit, but already he was getting used to it.

Normally, he slept in briefs. But now as he slid under the comforter and between the soft, cotton sheets, he didn't mind his nakedness. The cloth felt smooth against his abused flesh. The covers surrounded him. The pillow held his head positioned just right. Sleep began to envelop him before he took his next breath.

*

A distant beeping interrupted Wulf's dreams. Coming through a dense fog, his mind forgot his dreams as soon as he opened his eyes.

Light streamed through the window where the evening before he'd forgotten to close the curtains before getting into bed.

He pushed himself up on one elbow, his free hand rubbing at his eyes.

The beep sounded again to his right. On the night table sat a cell phone, its screen back-lit. He had not seen this phone before. Had someone come into his room — his cell — and left it in the middle of the night as he slept?

He shivered as he reached for it, lifting it toward his face so he could see it better. An answer light blinked green. Wulf touched it.

"Good," said a cool voice. Locke.

"I have a phone?" Wulf asked, voice hoarse from sleep.

"It only works as a two-way between you and me. All other functions but the clock are blocked. Don't think if you fiddle with it you can make those functions work. It's got alarms which are monitored by the guard stations."

Wulf had expected nothing more from the phone. It was the device itself that surprised him. Sleek. Black. Expensive. Like a gift he did not want.

When Wulf said nothing more, Locke's voice filled the silence.

"You are to rise now, shower and make yourself presentable. That includes shaving and combing your hair. It's a mess."

Wulf looked up to see if he could locate the camera that watched him. Or cameras, plural. For there had to be eyes all over his pretty cell. It was obvious Locke could see him live and in color even now.

"In one half hour you are to be ready to leave your rooms," Locke continued. "You may wear the shoes provided to you, or not. Your choice. But if you are not ready and clean and shaved, assistants will be sent in to force you to comply. It will not be enjoyable for anyone involved, most of all you. They are instructed to use the shock collar if need be."

Wulf had felt that pain only twice, and his mind already diminished the memory of it. But his physical self did not forget. Just the mention of the shock made his skin raise Goosebumps all over. His body shivered.

"Are my instructions clear?" Locke asked.

Wulf pressed the red spot on the screen to end the call. He did not like that Locke might think him stupid, but he was wise enough to hang up before he mouthed off about it.

He was ready to go in half the allotted time. The rest of the time he gazed out over the Palace grounds, looking at the empty platforms where, upon his arrival, live statues of men and women had stood.

He had no idea if playing statue was a part of training or punishment. All he knew was he didn't want to be one. These people—these Avilanians—had very strange ideas of art, life and philosophy. Dark ideas. Evil. To be a party to that—his mind wanted to rebel.

And yet the past twelve hours he'd been treated better than he had since he was caught. For that matter, he'd been pampered more here than he had ever experienced his whole life.

Even though he hated it, he knew he had been somewhat lucky to be chosen to come to the Palace. And Locke—well, Locke was another matter. The man confounded him. Locke owned him. Wulf should hate him. Instead, his stomach knotted. He found himself anticipating the day's events with both fear and curiosity. And Locke himself was interesting, at the very least.

All of it made Wulf outraged mostly at himself, but at least he wasn't in pain. He wasn't hungry. He was no longer tired. And his impending death had been put on hold.

He had not truly wanted to die. For that reprieve alone, he was grateful.

The door to his room/cell opened.

Locke stood at the threshold. "Ready?" he asked.

Wulf turned from the window. His body quickened at the sight of the Eminent Master, but he told himself it was simple apprehension. He had not forgotten Locke's appeal, a sort of glamour exuding from him that was more than his stature in the Palace. It came from within, an impeccable serenity, a magnetic soul. Wulf dismissed his anxious response to the man as culture shock, and disgust for what he represented.

"Are you asking if I am ready for a day of lessons in debauchery?" Wulf asked.

Locke raised one eyebrow. "Breakfast first, I should think."

Wulf pressed his lips tight, breathing deep through his nose.

"Hand me your leash."

Wulf looked down at the leather thong trailing over his chest. It reached just below his knees.

"Pick it up," Locke instructed. "Come forward. And hand it to me."

Wulf did not move.

"Did you hear me?"

Wulf stared at him, unblinking. But inside, his heart rate became rapid. He had no control here. Nothing left of his old self. Already it was happening, the body's reactions to fear and anger and despair overtaking him. He'd been trained not to give into these emotions. But with his life as he knew it gone—country, comrades in arms, even his clothing—past training meant nothing to his brain now. Less than nothing.

"You will not like it if I have to come to you and take the leash in hand myself," Locke warned.

Wulf's muscles went rigid. A last stand. He had so much defiance inside and nowhere to vent it.

Locke entered the room.

Wulf stood his ground, holding his breath, for if he let it out he knew he would start to gasp, to shake.

Locke grabbed the leash. Jerked.

Wulf grit his teeth. Shut his eyes.

The pain did not come.

Slowly, Wulf opened his eyes. "What happened?"

Locke looked at him with a steady brown gaze. "Nothing. I have your leash now. Will you come, or not?"

Wulf said, "The collar is not turned on?"

"Oh, the collar is on. Did you think it wasn't?"

"You pulled it. It didn't shock me."

"I did not pull. You projected in your mind that I would tug the leash once I had it in hand. Probably even felt a constriction at your neck, yes?"

Wulf glared at him. He did not like it that Locke seemed to be reading him as if they had already known each other for days, or even weeks.

"It's the conditioning of the collar. It works quite quickly, do you not agree? You haven't been here twenty-four hours and already you feel the collar's affects without me having to do a thing."

Anger surged in Wulf. "You won't do that to me!"

"Do what?"

"Condition me."

Locke sighed. "Everyone is conditioned in so many ways in life from the moment they are born. Even you. By your own culture, beliefs, habits, addictions, teachings. Through media we are told what to wear, to eat, speech mannerisms, how to style hair, clothing, and how to decorate our homes. Everything, and I mean everything, is conditioning."

Locke's words rolled past Wulf as garbled sound. He heard some of what he said, but didn't like it at all, and tuned the rest out, focusing instead on the man's face, which in itself was a mistake because the distraction of Locke, his beauty, made Wulf even more anxious.

One thing Wulf noticed—though he didn't want to-- was Locke's eyelashes were very thick and dark. Almost too pretty for a man. He wanted to turn away, but Locke had the leash now, and if he did pull back, the shock would come for sure.

"It is natural for you to tune me out on your first day when I say things you don't want to accept as truth. So for now, may we go to breakfast? The dining hall is out the door and to the right."

Wulf thought about the pain of the collar. If he pulled back and refused to accompany Locke, the knife-fire would consume him. How many times, he wondered, might he defy this master and stay sane? Or even conscious?

He thought he might try. But when Locke moved forward, Wulf's body followed, his heart racing. He could not do it. The memory of that pain was agony. His mind wanted to refuse. His body could not.

In Rille, his commander would have called him weak, a coward.

A sudden shudder came over Wulf.

Locke turned. His voice remained soft, commanding but not cruel, which was confusing. "You have my permission to take your time."

The gentleness of those words threw him into a quick fury that was gone as soon as it came. How effective it was, he thought. Keeping him off track, confused, unsure.

They entered the hallway at a slow walk. Wulf kept his gaze turned downward. He did not want to see other people, or know if they were looking at him. And if there were other slaves about, he did not want to see them.

But he could not shut off his other senses. He heart footfalls on marble tile. He felt the air flowing warm against his bare skin from light eddies and currents of those who passed by. The scents of other humans assaulted him, a combination of talc, sweat, spice, soap. People everywhere. People who were not his people, not his friends. The enemy.

Wulf paused.

As if reading his mind yet again, Locke paused along with him. He did not force Wulf to hurry. He did not jerk the leash. *Why?*

Wulf frowned.

"You're doing quite well," Locke said.

"Just shut up with your voice and… and all of it!" Wulf blurted.

He stood gasping now, hands clenched at his stomach, elbows in, body stiff. Wulf's eyelids fluttered. He squeezed them closed. The hallway was too noisy, too full, though he had actually seen no one about. But he'd heard them, smelled them.

"The option for me to shut up is not your choice to make. My voice is your beacon and you will obey it. You are experiencing anxiety. If it gets worse, we will see the doctor. For now, breathe out. Count to three. Do this until you feel yourself calm."

For some reason, Wulf did just that. It was automatic for the room had begun to spin and he was afraid if he fell the collar would activate.

Nothing was his to control anymore. Nothing.

Of course Locke was right. Wulf did not breathe in until the count of three. When he did, the world righted itself again.

He opened his eyes and the handsome master's eyes met his. Handsome. How could he think that? But his body responded. To his master. His *good-looking* master.

"Good," said Locke. "Do you like eggs? Bacon?"

"I don't want—" Wulf's voice stopped in his throat.

"I could enforce a diet on you." Locke soothed. "But I like to leave every slave I train with some choices. You may not be allowed to choose when you eat, but what you eat, within reason, can be made according to your tastes."

Probably this was another trick, Wulf told himself. But he did not like eggs at all. And he could not deny some consolation in the fact that he would not be forced to eat them.

The dining hall held an actual buffet. Wulf saw many naked slaves collared and leashed as he was following trainers about or sitting at tables and eating. Low volume instrumental music played, unobtrusive.

The artwork on the walls was more modern than what Wulf had seen in the rest of the Palace. These paintings were abstracts of bright shapes, or massive watercolor close-ups of flowers, more like pieces of scenes, or focused details of nature. He liked them.

Locke led Wulf to the buffet, saying, "You may choose whatever you like."

Wulf thought, *This is my training?*

But it was strange the way Locke's choice of words and actions encouraged instead of corrected. It was also infuriating, because in Wulf's deepest, darkest fantasies which he forbade himself ninety-nine percent of the time, Locke was his type.

Though half the room's occupants wore nothing, Wulf still could not get used to his own nudity. He faked an ease he did not feel, and had to consciously force himself from clasping his hands in front of his groin. Though he wanted to defy the culture of this so-called Palace, he did not wish to further display his vulnerability concerning it.

Wulf chose bacon and waffles for his breakfast. His hands shook as he held his tray.

Locke said nothing about Wulf's hands. In a hearty tone, he asked the cook to make him a fresh omelet.

When they approached a booth a booth with their food, a waiter laid a fresh towel on Wulf's couch before he sat. Locke used a hook on the wall to attach the leash.

The waiter then took their drink order, kneeling before Locke. The waiter himself wore only a white apron. Wulf couldn't help but notice he had been shaved to show off his strong, young chest and thigh muscles. A lovely man. He said, "Your drink, Master?"

"Coffee. Cream."

When the slave turned to Wulf, he called him, "Sir."

Wulf also ordered coffee.

"Surprised?" Locke asked.

"At what?"

"Everything."

"Of course. Nothing here is normal," Wulf replied.

Locke took a bite of his omelet. After he chewed and swallowed, he said, "What is normal?"

"All this, of course, is abnormal." Wulf gestured to the hall with a lift of his hand, and tried to keep the frustration from his voice.

"Perhaps you are correct." Locke nodded his head and continued in his infernally, gentle voice. "If I were in your country and had been captured by your soldiers, I would be imprisoned in a place not resembling this one in the least. It would not be normal to me, either."

"I was imprisoned. I am imprisoned!" Wulf insisted.

"What else is abnormal?"

"You took my clothes."

"You were born with no clothes, is that not normal?"

Wulf huffed. "You will use me — my body — for whatever sinful needs are deemed desirable by you people."

"The word sinful is a point of view, not a fact. And your body will not be used. It will be trained."

"For sex," Wulf put in. He stared at his food, not eating.

"For pleasure. As far as I know, pleasure is not bad word."

"Force is a bad word in conjunction with pleasure. Rape is a bad word." Wulf looked up, then down. He didn't want this conversation. He was being forced into this conversation.

Locke said, "If I were in a prison in Rille, would there not be force? And even rape?"

No prison in the world avoided such darkness. Wulf did not reply.

Locke calmly took another bite of his food. Then he said, "You are collared. Yes. You have no more rights. Yes. These things are true. But this Palace is a better fate than you could ever hope for. And you are under my protection. There will be no — uh," he shook his head wearily, "rape."

Wulf bristled at the man's denial. "You are a trainer of sex slaves. You *are* a rapist!"

Heads turned toward their direction from nearby tables. Wulf had not meant for the tempo of his voice to rise.

68

But what did he care? He had lost everything? He had nothing left.

"Everyone here at the Palace has signed a consent form."

"Except me," Wulf pointed out.

Locke contemplated him with steady brown eyes. He breathed in through his nose, quiet, seemingly unperturbed. "I have your signed consent form."

"It's faked."

"I see. Well, then. It's good you are not technically a Palace slave, then. I bought you. For now, you are mine. That is why you are here."

How could it be possible that the more Locke projected calm, the more Wulf experienced rage? He felt under threat from every corner, he just couldn't see it.

"But if you don't train me to be a pleasure slave, do you mean to eventually kill me after all? Then why put me through all this? Why?"

Locke started to open his mouth to respond, but Wulf didn't want to hear any more words from a man who was too beautiful to be a devil, but most certainly was. He wanted to smash those words from Locke's mouth. He wanted to shut him up with fists. His temper rose, quick and fierce.

Suddenly he could not hold himself back, all the fear and rage and anger burst through him. He lunged at Locke. Fast.

The leash pulled hard enough to break the hook away from its fastening on the wall.

The collar caught at Wulf with its own fury at the back of his neck on the spine. Fire and knives coursed through his body. It was as if he were being burned alive.

Wulf screamed and fell writhing to the floor.

The pain stopped within seconds but his body convulsed with the aftershocks.

The pain numbed all his thoughts for a few seconds, but when he returned to awareness he felt mortified. He was writhing, naked on the floor of a dining hall, *in front of spectators*. His mind could not contain this situation.

A voice said through the loud clanging of his pain, "Steady now." A hand touched his shoulder. Wulf flinched.

But Locke's palm pressed down on him until Wulf gave way, body relaxing on the cool tile one muscle at a time.

It seemed to take forever. But that hand stayed, firm and warm.

How many times over the past days in the prison, at the warehouse, at the auction, and here at the Palace had he pulled away from touch? This time he let the hand stay and could not say why. Except, he did not want to die. Thus, self-preservation had become of interest to him.

Wulf's eyes stung. His breathing came in frequent gasps and hitches. His ears still rang, drowning out most sound. After a moment, he heard Locke speaking as if he were far away. Occasional words.

"...not...different...sold...circumstance..."

He was speaking to him. Gentle. Calm. Damn him!

Wulf strained to put it all together, squeezing his eyes shut against his tears, and against the residual fire that still burned from his toes to his eyeballs, singeing him inside and out. The ringing in his ears diminished some. He began to hear full sentences.

"...no intention of killing anyone. Why would I spend a fortune for you simply to dispose of you?"

Wulf didn't know why Locke would do that. He didn't know anything anymore.

He opened his eyes and saw Locke kneeling over him, the leash sagging in his hand. A threat. But not a threat in this moment, for Wulf could not move.

"You are, in fact, safe here. If nothing else, try to understand that."

The man's definition of safety did not match Wulf's idea of that word.

"Just stop," Wulf heard himself mumble. "Just stop talking."

But if Wulf had learned anything in the past twenty-four hours, he understood that a slave could never order a master to do anything.

Chapter Nine – Locke

Such a waste. To see a beautiful specimen — and a seemingly intelligent one, at that — writhing on the floor on pain.

Locke was used to how the collar affected slaves in training, a necessary tool to remind the body and the individual within what might be expected of them. Most slaves enjoyed the collar, wanted it, because then they did not have to think, only do. Most slaves did not wear collars adjusted at any of the high settings. The shocks given as reminders to trainees were more like short, sharp nudges. Tiny jolts that almost tickled.

But Wulf had been labeled by every report on every computer. *Dangerous.*

Though Wulf belonged to Locke exclusively, Palace rules stated any slave with such a designation must wear their collar on one of several high modes. Locke agreed with the rule, though it rarely had to be implemented. For no one knowingly bought dangerous slaves-in-training here at the Palace.

Locke never thought to fight the rule regarding Wulf, for Wulf might be lovely and intelligent, but he was an unknown quantity.

Malik had called him untamed.

That word fit.

It was why they'd made their bet.

This amazing prisoner of war had come from a culture of fighters. And their enemy was anyone from Avilan. Simply, Wulf could not be trusted. At all.

And Locke had only nine days left to tame him.

Now he looked down at the suffering man before him, and began to hate that he had to use the collar on him to such a degree. He didn't train slaves to suffer. Of course, many slaves did suffer. At first. But none were like Wulf.

No one here continued in suffering unless they were mad, and then they were sent to hospital wards for help. The slaves trained. They learned. Everything from discipline to responsibility to manners. They learned structure, meditation, exercise and how to take care of their bodies inside and out. And then they learned how to use those perfect bodies. The side benefit was pleasure.

When they were sold to new masters, those masters were vetted. The slaves went to good homes. Rich homes. They lived in luxury with no worries, for the duration of their lives.

Wulf was different from all of them, though.

That was the reason Locke had purchased him.

Wulf's body had stopped trembling, but he kept blinking a little too hard and fast.

Locke said, "Can you sit up?"

Wulf behaved as if he'd just discovered his hands. The shock must have been a bad one. At the higher levels, the collar still dispensed its punishment in degrees depending on how it sensed the strength of tension in the slave, and the rapidity of a wrong move. It detected levels of violence in its wearer.

It was no surprise to Locke that Wulf had gotten angry and frustrated enough to want to lash out at him. Expected behavior, but Locke didn't have to like it.

He put his palm behind Wulf's shoulder and helped him sit up. Wulf had said not to touch him, but he didn't seem to notice this kind of touch.

The body of this man was like satin, and hot—so hot skin to skin, like caressing gentle flames when you'd been cold for a long, long time.

Even with the wind knocked out of him, Wulf outshone every slave in the dining hall with his bronze muscles, broad shoulders, and fool's gold hair. He was six-foot-three standing. Sitting on the floor did not diminish those numbers. Long and lean, but broad and strong enough to intimidate Special Forces soldiers, he was a treasure. Though trained to be focused on their own business, slaves — and even masters — let their attentions be distracted by Wulf's presence here in the hall. It would be no different anywhere else in the Palace. Wulf was that impressive.

Wulf's knees bent as he sat up straighter. The hair around his generously-sized cock glimmered. His cock was dark pink, and a softer blush of pink skin peeked out from the edges of the foreskin. He wasn't hard, he was just that well-endowed.

And the fight in this one!

Locke would have bought him even without a bet with Malik. Maybe he wouldn't even have tried to train him. Instead, he might have just kept him locked away, coddled and spoiled, a sculpted man to gaze upon after a hard day's work. Someone to hide away, tie up, pose like a doll.

He'd fantasized about keeping someone all to himself like that, under strict control.

But with Wulf's personality, holding him back like that, breaking him might destroy what captivated him about the man in the first place.

Looking at Wulf, Locke saw fantasies won and lost simultaneously.

Right now, nothing mattered but keeping this man with him. Making sure he stayed healthy. Sane.

It should have been simple.

After a few minutes, Wulf allowed Locke to help him up. The leash startled Wulf every time it went a little taut.

Locke led Wulf back to his seat. The hole in the wall where the leash-hook had been gaped, a long dark gash. Locke ignored the damage and signaled their waiter to take away their food, wipe away the bits of debris, and bring them fresh bacon, waffles, and coffee.

While they waited, Locke wound the end of the leash about his wrist, loose, then tilted his head and gazed at Wulf.

"We will eat," he said softly. "And then I will give you the tour."

Locke watched as Wulf glanced at the wall, staring at the hole he had made. Wulf's hands shook as he placed them, palms down, on the table.

Locke leaned forward a bit. Softer, "Look, I have no intention of killing you. Believe me or not. Your choice. But your status as a One-Night Thrall has been erased. You belong to me now. I decide what comes next for you."

For the duration of their breakfast, Wulf did not speak. For the first fifteen minutes, he did not eat. The collar might hurt badly, but it did not do physical, lasting damage. Still, he let Wulf settle into himself. He ordered more coffee, hot and fresh, and had the waiter take the cold cups away.

Finally, Wulf ate. In the end, he finished half his food and had one cup of coffee.

Satisfied that his new slave would not starve, and was strong enough to continue for the day, Locke led him on a tour.

He began with the exercise rooms.

Wulf followed without a word, but his head lifted at all the equipment they passed: weight machines, treadmills, cycles, rowers. He could tell Wulf was only pretending not to be impressed.

The room was half-filled to capacity. Some masters exercised alongside their slaves. Others were content to watch. A few trusted slaves, probably already graduated and simply awaiting placement, exercised alone.

The huge area led to the baths.

Wulf had learned his lesson in the dining hall and did not try to pull away, but he did lower his head.

Exercise was one thing. Bathing naked was another. Perhaps to Wulf bathing was instilled in him to be a more private affair. Here in the Slave Palace, it wasn't. Especially in these public baths, where more than bathing was going on.

Some slaves and masters of both genders lounged naked and relaxed in the hot pools, their jets bubbling the clear water. Others swam in the larger, cooler pool at the center. A few had secluded themselves on benches under leafy potted plants, or on corner steps of smaller pools, and were enjoying oral sex. They were somewhat discreet, but it might be a shock to an over-sheltered Rilleian like Wulf.

Locke did not stare directly at Wulf to gauge his reactions, but he did keep an eye on him. For this was only the beginning, and acclimating Wulf to his new life was paramount on Locke's mind.

For Locke, public sex and nudity was normal. He gave it no extra thought. The act of sex was natural to him, like eating. But he did understand inhibition in new trainees, and shyness, and culturally programmed restraint. A man like Wulf had to be all bound up inside. Locke looked forward to untying those knots.

For now, Wulf kept his gaze turned downward, his hanks of golden hair hiding his cheeks and jaw.

To get his attention, Locke turned his attention away from the pools. "The mosaics on the walls are done by a team of artists known as the Dawns of Time. They use tile, gemstones, glass and ceramic in their art."

Wulf finally glanced up through his fallen bangs at the nearest windowless wall. It contained swirls of color depicting humans frolicking with mermaids and mermen. A few dolphins looked on from the wall's edge.

Locke pointed to the wall in front of them, past two hot pools, one of which held a quite randy slave tipping his master up by the hips and swallowing his cock whole.

Locke pretended not to see them, and said, "That one took months to do."

The mosaic was an orgy of bodies, buttocks, cocks, breasts, and spread legs so intricately done it looked three-dimensional.

Wulf's only response was a fast, loud breath through his nose, almost a snort. But a soft pink tint came to his cheeks.

Locke noted it with not a small amount of pleasure. Everything about Wulf caught his attention and made his body tight, hot, distracted.

"We can come back to these rooms later for a work-out and a soak, perhaps." Locke did not phrase it as a question.

But Wulf lifted his chin slightly and turned his head, not meeting Locke's eyes. "Are you asking if I want to?"

"No," Locke replied. "If I ask you what you want, I will be very clear on the matter."

Wulf's lips turned down. An ordinary slave might have gotten a light rebuff for that behavior — making a face at a master's words. Wulf was no ordinary slave.

Locke ignored the pout and lifted the leash, the gold chain glittering in the bath lights reflected off the glimmering pool waters.

Locke thought about where to take Wulf next. The Palace had everything, a mall with intriguing shops, an adult school, a theatre and a bowling alley. But he remembered Malik and the bet. He was wasting time. Although Wulf was one he wanted to treat delicately, Locke's bet with Malik left him little time to dally. Yesterday counted as day one. Today was day two. After that, only eight days remained to tame the wild beast.

He told himself he didn't care about the money. But the bet — that was about pride and saving face. He didn't want to admit it, but losing annoyed him. He might be an Eminent Master, but he was not immune to being shallow about some things in life.

Bets with Malik ranked high on that list.

"I think we will go to the training rooms next," Locke said.

Wulf's body stiffened.

"This way," Locke ordered.

To avoid another shock, Wulf had no choice but to follow.

Locke enjoyed his job. When another person was vulnerable and waiting for Locke to instruct their next move, he could not deny a cool, sexual thrill. The power play dynamic was etched into his veins. Control. Dependency. Need. Want. All these things mixed together in his mind to produce a tingle on his skin and a burn deep inside.

But most of the time, his heart was not involved. This was how he was taught to be a good master. Don't get too close. The dependency of the slave toward the master grew fast and must be curtailed. It wasn't a problem for Locke. This was a job. For new slaves, there could be pouting, frustration, anger, and tears. For trained masters, none of those emotions were allowed to exist.

This was all different and new for Locke. Wulf was his. A personal purchase. A friendly bet. A man whose beautiful body and fierce personality intrigued him so much it had him hesitating in his usual, easy-going manner. And questioning all of his perfectly trained moves.

He needed to get hold of himself. But then again, he wasn't sure he wanted to.

The training rooms were not far. They were on an upper level of the back wing of the palace. A wide marble staircase let to them. Red carpet adorned the center of the stairs, as if one were climbing to an ethereal throne room, or a realm of absolute authority. The walls gleamed with gold framed paintings of erotic scenes of humans, fauns, fairies, and satyrs fucking in various ways. Some light, some dark, they depicted the sensuous worlds of sexual desire, passion, lust and pleasure.

That any culture might teach something was wrong in the expression of pure natural ecstasy boggled Locke's mind.

Wulf's thigh muscles flexed as he ascended the stairs, tightening to show off the rigid edge of muscle on the sides. He would be hard down there, like satin over steel but warm and, if well-oiled, slippery. And Locke hadn't even gotten to thinking about that generous cock. The thighs were what he wanted to feel along the palms of his hands, to touch and caress.

And maybe the biceps as well, yes, most certainly the biceps. And the area just beside the armpit. That was one of Locke's favorite places to caress a lover. Lover? What was he thinking? This was a slave. And yet, *his* slave. He could do and think whatever he wanted about him.

It was obvious Wulf had worked out every day of his adult life.

Locke wanted to say something to prepare Wulf for the training room. He decided against it. Nothing he did would prepare this man who emphatically believed sex and pleasure slaves were a grave sin.

The double doors stood twelve feet high. They opened automatically as Locke waved his palm over the small square security screen. This was not a public place. Slaves did not enter on their own here without a leash and without a master. Nor were they left unattended in this room. Only masters could come and go from this room at will.

The square of the security pad lit up pink and yellow to acknowledge Locke. Then it started to bleed green from the edges. When the screen filled with green light, the doors slowly swung open to the inside.

Locke walked across the threshold with Wulf trailing only inches beside and behind him.

The room was vast, set with alcoves left and right along each wall. At the center of the room a long runway-like stage ran all the way to the back wall, which was about one hundred feet. That stage contained steps every few feet so it was easy to climb up and down.

Masters used it to view their slave's balance, walk, form, composure. They could stand or sit below the stage and observe their slave from every angle, order them to squat, kneel, sit, lie down. Slaves learned more than just sex acts. They were taught how to perform for their future master's pleasure, everything from dancing a strip-tease to how to offer their bodies in the most sumptuous of ways.

Right up front two resplendent slaves, one male, one female, moved and swayed to their masters' orders.

About fifteen feet down, a third male slave knelt, ass up in the air, forehead touching the floor of the stage. He was well-oiled, his brown skin shining, his black hair reflecting almost blue in the light from the high skylights in the thirty-foot-high ceiling.

Out the corner of his eye, Locke saw Wulf's eyes widen at the displays before him.

Locke waited until Wulf noticed the big screens above the alcoves. They flickered and flashed. Impossible not to draw the eye. The screens depicted close ups of all manners of erotic acts. The masters could control what was played upon them. In fact, there was one class being taught at the end of the room and Locke could see that the master controlled a group of six men and was focused on teaching them the art of male to male fellatio. The master kept gesturing to the big screen overhead where they stood. The screen showed the close-up of an erect penis being licked and swallowed by an eager, plush-lipped mouth.

It was a known fact that video aided greatly not only in the teaching of techniques before they were implemented upon a real person, but in arousal as well.

When Wulf finally looked up at the screens, his lips parted. It seemed he held his breath for a very long time before finally expelling it and looked downward, as was his habit.

"There is no shame in the training room. This is a safe space," Locke said.

But Wulf's face was already flushed, and he shifted his feet nervously as his cock bounced a little, slightly springier than his usual uninterested state.

Locke suppressed a smile. Well, well, Wulf was human after all.

Not that Locke had ever doubted it.

Chapter Ten – Wulf

"Walk with me," Locke said, lifting Wulf's leash higher as he raised his arm.

Afraid that even the slightest tug that might set off the collar's shock mechanism, Wulf stumbled forward.

The men and women on the long stage were without leashes, and he saw the long chains curled into neat piles on the floor. Wulf longed for his to be removed even if the collar stayed. He'd become afraid of any trip or fumble that might punish him. Locke was not careless with the leash, but he didn't trust him.

Nor did Locke trust Wulf, obviously. His mind schemed at how he might get Locke to remove the leash without it looking like he was ever going to succumb to this evil place and its ways and rules.

He supposed he could simply ask. But pride swelled his throat and he'd been swallowing most of his words for days before arriving at the Slave Palace, preferring silence as one method of rebellion.

He moved alongside Locke without a word, unable to do anything else.

Locke gestured with his free hand to the alcoves that lined the walls. Was Wulf was supposed to look into them? Obviously, Locke wanted him to see everything in here.

And so he did. Each alcove had a red-covered bed against the wall, made up neatly with pillows and extra cushions. Above the bed was a large mirror framed by red velvet curtains. The mirror could be covered or not according to a master's whim. There was room around the bed for a person to walk, stand, or sit with their legs stretched out.

The first three alcoves on either side of the room were unoccupied as Wulf and Locke walked by.

But the next alcoves contained couples. Why Wulf had not heard their groans of pleasure until now was a mystery, but now he could see and hear. The first two contained both males and females. One was a female master with a male slave. The other, a male slave with a female master.

Locke kept walking until the next alcoves revealed their occupants. Male couples. Both alcoves revealed they were participating in anal intercourse. In one alcove, the master, wearing only his black shirt, was fucking his male slave doggie style. In the next, the master lay on his back on the bed while the naked slave he was training bounced enthusiastically on his erect cock, doing all the work.

Wulf preferred men in his own private fantasies — not that Locke had ever asked — but that orientation was considered an abomination in his culture.

Wulf didn't realize he was staring, licking his lips, until Locke made a sound like a satisfied sigh beside him.

He closed his mouth and glanced straight ahead. But that didn't help, either, for there was a group of men at the far end of the stage being instructed in oral sex. Half were kneeling while the other half was standing, their erect members poking in an out of willing mouths. Evidently, some masters used other slaves to train slaves in the art of pleasure — on each other.

Locke seemed — infernally! — to always be reading his thoughts. It was no different now when Locke said, "There are classes in the sexual arts which some masters teach to more than one student at a time. It's effective to have them practice on each other so they can understand first hand how things feel both giving and receiving pleasure."

Wulf glanced again at his own feet. But even then he wasn't safe from this madness. His own cock was becoming tumescent. The pink tip had already poked free of the foreskin. His balls began a distinct but still distant ache.

"Just as you had to remove all your clothes to enter into this world as not a prisoner but a slave, you must now open your eyes. If you face your fears, they become less scary," Locke said.

It was all nonsense. Ridiculous. Facing one's fears. Becoming a pleasure slave. A pleasure slave! It was pure insanity.

"I could order you to join that class," Locke said softly.

"No!" It was the first word he'd said in a while, and it blurted out of him, an intonation of harsh denial.

But how could he not wonder at what it might feel like—a tongue on his balls, lips kissing the glans of his cock. Already his mind was being brainwashed. It couldn't be this easy to become corrupted. It couldn't!

"Are you afraid of having the act done to you, or doing it to someone else?" Locke asked.

"Neither." But his answer wasn't entirely honest. He was nervous. Where he came from, sex was treated with sanctity, a sacred event, and very private. Never talked about much. "It is an act to be revered, not like this, a... a desecration."

"Nowhere else on the planet is it revered more than here in this palace," Locke replied. "We treat the art of pleasure *as* art. We teach it as art. It is cherished. Honored. Above reproach. Not something to be ashamed of. Not a wicked transgression. Or a sin."

"That is fine for all those who wish to be here. I do not wish to be here." Wulf could not help but see his plight as a crime.

"Yes, for you everything is different."

Wulf glanced up from the floor to Master Locke's dark eyes. They glimmered in the light, as if laughing at him.

"Do not mock me."

Locke blinked. "That is not my intent."

Feeling bold, he asked, "What is your intent?"

"Everything you've done and said and every move you've made since the moment you arrived is helping me decide that very thing."

"You don't already know?"

Locke gave him a strange smile. Not mocking. "Even now, I am still deciding."

"What to do with me," Wulf finished.

"Yes."

"You saved my life. You must have a reason."

Locke said, "Come," and tugged at the leash, still slack, but making Wulf more nervous nevertheless. He matched strides with the master.

Locke led Wulf into an alcove. Like the others, it contained a curtained mirror, a bed, and a cabinet enclosing a sink. Just beyond the bed, in one corner hidden by an extension of the mirror's curtain, was a toilet.

It was a jail cell. At least, that's how Wulf viewed it. He did not see the point of the alcoves. For privacy, training could be done in bedrooms like the one Wulf had been given. If this was for public display, why the cozy trappings?

The alcove was fastidiously clean, the coverings on the bed crisp and smelling of fresh laundry detergent.

Locke pointed at the bed. "Sit."

Wulf did not move.

"Go ahead," Locke said.

"Why?"

Locke's brows narrowed.

"What are you going to do?" Wulf asked.

Locke stood at the foot of the bed. With a casual flip of his hand, he let his grip on the leash relax. The end of the chain fell making a soft chiming sound as it hit the floor. He placed his gloved hands behind his back, and faced Wulf.

Once more, he said, "Sit."

Wulf looked at the end of the leash where the ring of it glittered against the shining tile. Finally, he decided it couldn't hurt to sit.

The bed was soft against his naked buttocks. He placed his hands, one on top of the other, in his lap right above his groin, the sides pressing his abdomen.

Locke continued to stand, now looking down at him. The change in their positions was not lost on Wulf, for now he was no longer "taller" than Locke.

"Now," Locke said. "You asked me a question."

"What are you going to do?"

"No. The earlier statement. Why did I save your life."

Wulf huffed and looked straight ahead at the cabinet and its in-set sink.

"Look at me, please, when I talk to you."

"Oh? I'm not supposed to keep my eyes downcast?" Wulf asked.

"No. I have not asked that of you, have I?"

Wulf turned his gaze on Locke. Frowning.

Locke continued. "The truth of the matter is you hooked me."

More frowning.

"You caught my attention. The moment you came onto the stage, you exuded not only your obvious beauty," and here he paused with a quick wave of his hand, "but an energy, a power churning within you. Magnificent, actually. And I was just shallow enough and bored enough in that moment to be completely taken in."

Wulf hated every word this master said. More, he hated hearing the sounds right outside the alcove coming from the stage, and from the other alcoves, and the class. Moans. Groans. Grunts. Some shouts. Some laughter. And yet, he could not quite hate Locke. Deep inside, a hesitation occurred, confusing him. The handsome master and his low, calm voice quickened his intrigue.

"You bought me because you were bored?" Wulf asked.

Locke let out a chuckle. "I consider myself an artist. I saw the canvas and the paints and saw potential."

86

"So you didn't save my life because I am a human being."

"Oh, that, too. I don't believe in killing slaves for any reason, even if they are crazy. One-Night Thralls are for underworld crime lords and back alley deals. Criminal."

"So are you saying you save every dangerous thrall that crosses your path?"

"No. I wish I could. I am saying I saved you."

Wulf still didn't understand why he had *hooked* Locke other than that he was considered beautiful.

"And now," Locke said, "you are wondering what that entails. I am showing you my home, my kingdom."

"You are king?"

Locke laughed again. An easy tone. It unnerved Wulf.

"Some may see it that way," Locke said.

"You are king," Wulf said. "And now I am yours. Your slave. That is how it is. And you want me to act like the other slaves here. The only difference, I am not to be sold. I will remain. Yours. To answer your every beck and call."

"That isn't the only difference. They all consented to be here. You did not. So what to do with you becomes a new detail for me to ponder."

"An insignificant detail, I assume." Wulf's tone lowered in disgust.

"No. It's significant. I could rescind the contract based on the forgery of your consent. But that would mean you would go back to prison. For life. You might even be found too dangerous to hold, and be put to death. It would be a full lock-down prison for dangerous and violent offenders. It would not be a pleasant life, or a long one probably. And now that I've bought you and read your file and looked you over—"

"—And got hooked by my looks on the stage—" Wulf interrupted.

"Yes. That. There's a challenge for me where you are concerned. I like a challenge."

"Because you were bored."

"Maybe. But I have always loved challenge. All those reasons keep me from throwing away the contract and returning you, as I would have every right to do. And I think you also know that you are in a better position because of me. Even if you don't yet trust me."

"Trust?" Wulf asked. "You are actually using that word with me?"

"Why not? I have invited you, a stranger, into my home. I have made sure you have everything you need to be comfortable and healthy. I have saved your life from being used, abused and thrown away as a One-Night Thrall. I have promised not to re-sell you. I'm not sure what more you need from me to gain your trust?"

"I'm not saved by you, but taken against my will," Wulf protested. But Locke's words made his thoughts scramble until he was not sure of his position.

As a warrior, there had always been the possibility of being taken by the enemy. Captured. Against his will. It was the risk he took—a risk everyone in his regimen took—when they fought their challengers. Wulf's country had a draft.

Though Wulf had signed up for combat training of his own free will, he had felt he had no choice. He had been taught he must fight against the enemy, the evil he'd grown up fearing. Plus, he could find no better way to escape his abusive father. There had never been a time he was not reminded of how terrible so much of the world was, and told that as a true citizen he should fight against that wickedness.

This man before him, Locke, was a part of that wickedness. A challenger. A saboteur of good. This was what his mind was telling him even as his heart vacillated.

Wulf had been staring at his feet. Hating the softness caressing his buttocks. Despising this so-called training room with all its perversions meant for only one thing: Sex. Debauchery. Fucking.

Now he glanced aside through the veil of his hair to see Locke standing before him, all in black, hands held behind his back.

Wulf could take this man down in seconds. His height and strength were his advantage. Combat training had made him strong. But only physically. His mental strength—his will—was separate. This part of him had been trained as well toward unquestioning patriotism and loyalty, and a denial of all things his culture defined as sin. The list was easy to memorize.

The rules of obedience straight-forward and succinct. But they had nothing to do with his feelings, and his heart. In fact, the rules denied the heart in favor of pure obedience. And now here he was again in the center of a world that demanded pure obedience. His life depended upon it.

Locke stood before him, yet one more general ready to command. But this one saw to a few things others never had before. Wulf's comfort, for one. Back home, after he'd left his father and become an independent adult, no one cared about him. Not even his companions in the dormitories. He lived to fight, as they did. They ate together and slept together, but only because the situation required it. Not because they wanted to, or cared much for each other beyond having a sparring partner or two.

Wulf hadn't been in the Slave Palace twenty-four hours and his trainer acted as if he did care. Making promises. Keeping patience with Wulf's temper.

But it was all probably an illusion. He was one more cog in a machine to be ordered around by others.

Still, it was a pretty machine. Locke was of the build and coloring and bearing that fueled Wulf's fantasies. Dark hair and eyes, sun-browned skin, a lithe body that moved with grace and little effort. Hands with long fingers that held his leash, although that leash lay limp at his side as if all under Wulf's control now.

And Locke's voice. Like velvet sliding across his mind, inviting. He might, if he allowed himself, roll into that voice, bask in it.

What might a man with utter patience like Locke, an Eminent Master, be like to know, to obey? To touch?

Wulf shook his head hard, averting his gaze to his feet again. He could not allow himself such thoughts. It was wrong. But wrong by whose standards? Whose teachings? Even the voice in his head that asked those questions made him so uncomfortable his mind swam.

All Wulf's musings seemed pointless.

Locke said, as if there had been no pause, "I understand you do not feel you have been saved from any fate. That this is your fate now, and hopefully not something you must endure."

"Isn't it?" Wulf did not look up this time.

"I would not have it be so," Locke replied.

Wulf was surprised. How could Locke say such a thing?

"If you would talk to me, help me learn about you," Locke said, "I could maybe help this be less of an endurance for you."

"Learn about me?" Wulf's voice came out low, soft. "You will keep me as a slave no matter what. Keep me naked and leashed. What else would you need to know about me? Beyond that, I am nothing. I am not what matters."

"Hmm. Interesting." Locke made a noise as if taking a long, deep breath. "You are not what matters, you say. That is a statement you make that you believe in. Correct?"

"Of course." Wulf nodded numbly.

"What if I told you it was false. What if I could make you see that you matter a lot."

"As a pleasure slave?" Wulf let out a hiss of disgust.

"Yes. Because as a pleasure slave you hold the power of want and desire over another."

"But I have no recourse to say yes or no, so I have no power," Wulf replied. This conversation was laughable.

"Oh, but with the right master, you most certainly do."

Wulf's brow creased. His head began to ache more than the residual effects of the shock at breakfast.

He didn't want to ask. But what could Locke mean by "the right master?"

As if reading his question straight from his mind, Locke said, "You will learn things here just as you learned how to use a weapon in your training to be a good soldier. Think of this as yet one more tool for your arsenal, the ability to seduce, to give pleasure, and to receive it as well to complete the wholeness of your being."

"Ridiculous," Wulf said. Allowing himself to be raped was a tool?

"Not ridiculous. An art. A trade. A technique. People have won wars with just one kiss," Locke said.

Wulf wanted to laugh. Instead, he forced small breaths in and out of his nose and mouth. His cock had betrayed him, but he could not see that as power. Not yet. Maybe never. To him, it was a weakness.

"I want you to do something for me."

"You are asking?" Now Wulf looked up, his hair flying back.

His neck felt hot and now coolness descended there where his skin was bared. He had felt hot ever since he came into the alcove. But somewhere air filtered through to where Locke was standing and Wulf was sitting, fluttering against his skin.

"I am telling you what I want," Locke replied. "And the sooner you do it, the easier it will be for you to get along here. To exist here."

"With you," Wulf added.

"Yes. With me. I do own you."

Wulf had never, for one moment, forgotten that fact.

"I want you to look closely at everything in this training room. Everything. From the people and classes, to the videos on the upper walls and the activities of the people in the other alcoves."

"Why do you want me to look at that?" Wulf asked. "It's humiliating to me. It does not help me in my situation."

"When you look, when you see closely what is happening around you, and how what might be a mystery to you works, how it is prepared for, how it is done, what happens to the person, the body, the mind… then your fears will diminish. It is no different from breathing, eating. Learning to walk. Or learning to fight."

"It is not like fighting!"

"No?" Locke questioned. "To learn of pleasure is a great reward. That is why this Palace exists."

"And what of—" Wulf stopped. He was going to say *love*. It was a word he knew only in relation to familial love, which he had not known, or loyalty to a cause. He'd never experienced any other kind of love. He'd never fallen in love. In fact, he wasn't sure he even believed in that sort of thing. Locke might be his "type" but what did that have to do with love?

"What of?" Locke prompted.

Wulf shook his head.

"I will answer any question you have to the best of my ability."

"Your rank says your ability is the best."

"It is. But I am also human. I don't know everything."

"No?" Wulf countered not without some sarcasm.

"No."

Wulf hung his head.

"What was it you wanted to ask?" Locke said.

He hesitated. He could not deny his frustration. But Locke seemed so smug. Casual. And Wulf, a mere slave, wanted to dare himself. Wanted to ask what maybe no slave should ever ask.

"Do you teach about love here?"

"Ah, now that is a great question. And very important. Possibly the most important question you could ever ask me."

Wulf saw the smile curve the corners of Locke's pink lips, how it plumped the cheeks and made the skin look smooth and taut all at once transforming the harder edged planes of his face to a thing of beauty.

He must not think these things! Must not!

To Wulf's further humiliation, his face and then his whole body began to heat. He wished he could take back his words right now. It didn't help him in his blushing dilemma when Locke's voice washed over him, using that word — love.

"Yes, we teach about love here. There are endless novels, essays and poems on the subject. Paintings, sculptures, plays, songs. It's endless. The answer is yes. And yes. We teach it. We teach it because everything we do from the moment we take our first breaths as infants until the day we die should be about it, for any way of life without some love — everything from work to play — is a crime to us. And maybe — maybe one day, you will understand this."

"What makes you think I don't?"

Locke gave him a smile Wulf could only describe as enigmatic. "Because you are so young."

"I am twenty-three."

"As I said."

"You must also assume it is because I am from Rille, a country that was enemy to your country. Because we are not as… as promiscuous as you are in this country, you must assume--"

"No," said Locke, interrupting. His eyebrows scrunched together. "I attempt to not make assumptions that are so generalized. But I am not perfect. If you think I have made assumptions about you, I apologize."

It did occur to Wulf that he was making his own assumptions. But he was the slave, not the master. He had no choices. He felt a bit justified in being a hypocrite.

"This is your first day," Locke continued. "There is so much that will be strange to you, perhaps even frightening."

"Humiliating—" Wulf put in.

"Perhaps. But if you are unsure about your future, and all that is around you, it can produce great anxiety."

Wulf let out a hard breath, making a sound of protest. But of course Locke was correct. Anxiety. Depression. Anger. How could he not have them all? He was a prisoner of war. Now a slave. That would never change.

For solitary moments, and maybe during sleep, he might escape the notion of what he was, and erase the bars those labels drew in his mind, but escape was not an option. Ever. Not as long as he had no assets—or clothing of his own. Not as long as he had the shock-collar.

"Now," Locke said, still standing with his hands clasped, his posture straight and tall. "You will begin your sex lessons here today. Lie back."

"What?" Wulf tossed his head back, feeling his hair scrape the skin of his naked back. When he tilted his face up, he scented an odor of sweetness on the air, like baking cookies.

"Do as I say, please."

"Or you'll shock me with the collar?"

Locke did not answer. He leaned down and fiddled with something at the end of the bed which Wulf could not see.

Wulf did not move.

At last, Wulf heard a click. The bed vibrated a bit. His body jerked in surprise, but it was nothing to be afraid of. He watched as a small platform rose up, and on it was a flat, thin screen, wide as the bed.

A computer? A television?

Locke came around to the side of it and touched the screen a few times. Visuals appeared.

"Am I to watch a movie?"

"Yes," said Locke. "And when you are done there will be a test."

Wulf wanted to laugh. In fact, he felt his mouth open, and the corners of his lips quirked up.

Locke said, "You may relax as you watch. Lean against the pillows. I also give you permission to enjoy yourself, if you'd like."

"What?"

"You may masturbate. I will allow it."

"You will allow — ?" He gulped.

"You will watch the entire film. You will not leave this alcove. Your collar's leash may not be attached to anything, but if you attempt to leave this area, I will see. I will engage the collar."

Wulf shook his head. "Lovely. Thank you for this opportunity to self-pleasure myself while I watch pornography." He drew out the words to further lace them with his sarcasm.

As if he did not notice Wulf's tone, Locke simply said, "You're welcome."

"You will be watching me." Wulf did not phrase it as a question.

"Of course. I will not lie to you. There are cameras everywhere in the Palace. Nothing is not seen."

After Locke spoke, he turned away from Wulf and moved beyond the right wall of the alcove, leaving Wulf's sight.

For a moment, Wulf had the urge to get up, to follow him. He had been alone in his rooms all night, but this was different. Though he had minor privacy in the alcove, this was still a public area. A training room where masters and slaves passed through at all hours. He could even hear them coming and going, and the muffled gasps and laughter from the class still taking place at the far end of the hall.

Next door, more grunts and moans and thumps wafted on the air. The alcove walls were too thin to muffle anything.

Wulf looked down at the bed. Fluffy pillows—ivory, and lavender—decorated the red bed. Some were square throw pillows; others were long, tube-shaped, soft body-pillows. They could be stacked or spread out, arranged any way he pleased.

The video began to play, soft music lulling from its mechanized structure.

Wulf's eyes were drawn to it as if he had no control. For that was what light screens—computers, TVs, phones—were like. Hypnotic. He'd been away from that sort of thing in his warrior training except for educational purposes, or purposes of communication. Rille's computers and phones were not accessible to any Internet services. They were programmed only with that which his government deemed proper and necessary for them to see.

Wulf had seen pornography anyway, of course. Once or twice in his life. There were always hackers in one group or another. Always boys—and even some girls—who loved to be upstarts, to disobey, to keep secret stashes of taboo movies or books. Every country in the world had a black market.

But he had not lingered if friends showed him forbidden material. Wulf had always been too nervous about repercussions. His country was known for its violence, even against its own peoples. Not that they didn't deserve what was coming to them—or so he was told.

The music began as a prelude. The visuals on the movie began, with a soft narrative, male voice explaining what the movie promised.

First the voice, almost like Locke's but not quite as dulcet, addressed the viewer directly.

"Find a comfortable place. Relax your body. Open yourself to a world of pleasures. This film will instruct not only your mind in technique and pleasure-giving, but teach the body as well. Give yourself permission to respond. To react. This is part of your lesson in the art of love-making, erotic sex, and pleasure into the realm of ecstasy."

96

Wulf did not want to relax or respond. Locke had said cameras were everywhere. That he was watched. He said, aloud, looking up at random areas of the ceiling and walls, "I thought you were the Eminent Master. I thought you were the teacher, not a machine. If you teach through videos, why do you masters even exist?" He almost spat the last word.

There was no response, of course.

The movie began with an almost anatomical description of males and females.

Aloud, Wulf said, "I understand general anatomy."

He could not help but be offended. He most certainly did not need a lesson on the fact that males had penises and females had vaginas. It was an insult.

But the film did not delay, or linger on simplistic matters. That introductory part took less than a minute.

The film then began to show, as if in glorified celebration, how men and women existed to procreate with one another, but pleasure in and of itself was not defined by procreation. Thus, any pairing was acceptable, any grouping from two or more a lovely thing, and it was a slave's purpose to understand that any and all aspects of lovemaking might be expected of them, and they were to show no prejudice toward any of them.

Well, that was ridiculous. How could Wulf ever accept things he was disgusted by?

The film started off showing the most ordinary of couplings, explaining them in great detail. Males with females. How their anatomy worked together.

Wulf was bored. He had not moved from his seat on the side of the bed. Had not touched a pillow or adjusted his legs. But even though male/female sex was not his true, deep fantasy, he could not help but be affected.

His body tensed. He felt little darts of electricity in his abdomen. And he noted that his mind was drawn to the men in the film, their firm bodies, their erect cocks.

The film showed women together. The explanations became a monotone to him.

But when men were shown with men, kissing, touching, he wanted to look away.

He glanced up to the ceiling again, trying to discern where any cameras might be.

The muscles in his back began to flutter and ache from sitting in one position so long. He lifted a knee as if to fold his leg underneath himself upon the bed for more comfort, then pushed it back off the bed, the sole of his foot hitting cool tile again.

He took a deep breath as the two male models on the screen kissed. The narrator talked about the art of kissing and foreplay. Not everything was about the actual act of fucking.

"I don't want to watch this," Wulf said glumly.

But his eye was drawn. The two men were beautiful, one blond, one brunet, sporting similar colorings and race to himself and Locke.

Wulf closed his eyes. The electric flurries in his stomach sent trickles of sensation to his balls. His cock elongated against his will.

Wulf drew his legs up and flopped onto the bed, cushioned by the pillows on his side, facing the counter and sink, not looking at the TV at all.

But the voice on the TV droned on with words such as "lips" and "tongue" and "sucking" and "arousal." It talked of more than sex, using words like "intimacy" as well. And "communication," "chemistry," "connection."

There were harder words, too, words Wulf did not care about or understand about how the brain functioned when in arousal, and how the mind formed associations and connections which the body acted out.

"Because of its damp warmth and muscle strength," the voice said, "the tongue is able to create erogenous zones on parts of the body one might never think of as erotic. Placing the tongue on the glans of the penis creates great pleasure in most..."

Wulf's head shot up. He had seen the heterosexual coupling include oral sex, but toned it out. No details had invaded his mind. But the men together pressed onto his brain. He did not want to look at the screen and watch one beautiful model orally stimulate the other beautiful model.

But it was as if he had no will! His eyes sought the screen.

The narrator's voice went into his mind like a bell awakening him from slumber. The words meant nothing on their own. However, combined with the beauty of the images on the screen, Wulf's cock became fully erect.

A man sucking another man's cock: Wulf hardly ever allowed himself to think of it, for his body always—always!—betrayed him, and he liked control over himself.

No, he could not imagine it. Which was why the lessons at the far end of the training hall on fellatio had made him squirm. And why he'd panicked when Locke had made the simple suggestion that he could join in that class.

His cock filled. There were cameras everywhere, though he could not see them. Locke would know. Locke would know his deepest, darkest secret that this act turned him on. That this act made him a true slave. To body. To mind. To the sin of uncontrollable, forbidden sexual bliss.

Wulf groaned. "Fuck you," he said aloud.

His eyes darted back and forth from the sink to the screen, watching the teasing tongue on the erect penis, the way the lips pressed the head of the swollen organ, how they sucked the flesh slowly, as if it were a delicacy to be savored. How the mouth moved all the way down on the cock. The model's cheeks hollowed as he began to suck and move slowly up the shaft, then down.

Wulf could not breathe. This was why he did not look at pornography. He detested this out-of-control feeling. He wanted to hone his body as a tool, not see it perform anything against his will. If his body did not do as he commanded, he considered it a mistake on his part. A failure.

Now, he watched the movie and leaned back against the soft pillows. His hand pushed his cock down until he could trap it between his thighs. He would ensnare his cock, trap it, bind it into submission.

Back home, he had a device he used for such times. Everyone called it a petal. All boys had one from an early age. If things were out of hand "down there" you simply wrapped your penis in the soft sheath of the petal. A chain attached to the top was brought backward between the legs, pulling the offending member down and back against the testicles. The chain could be adjusted to hook tightly to side loops in Rilleian underwear. It made things easy, contained, not embarrassing.

He had no petal. In fact, the country of Avilan had probably never heard of them, unless they used them in kinky escapades for orgasm denial on purpose for furthering pleasure and not to deny it as the sin it was.

Wulf clamped his thighs tight, but his cock was too tumescent now, beginning to throb, and had a mind of its own. It popped out into the sweet-scented air. He would have to use his hands to hold it back.

He had trained himself from a very young age not to touch himself. It was considered by his culture a sin. But now there was no petal. Only the brutal and naked grip of a hand.

He hated himself right now. He hated everyone and everything. But he could not stop his reality. The video continued to play. There was nothing to be done but grasp himself and push down, push his erection between his legs, clamp his thighs, and hold his hand there.

The insides of his thighs were damp. His palm sweated. Everything was too slippery. And far too bright, the lights, the TV screen flickering, the frustration behind his eyes making them ache.

He closed his eyes but the voice in the film became more and more explicit, and Wulf's imagination conjured images as if he were watching the film. It did not make a difference.

He cracked an eyelid when the voice described how the peak of pleasure rose to culminate in orgasm.

He saw the stiff penis in the mouth of the beautiful model, as well as the other model's body taut and arched, his muscles standing out in relief beneath toned skin—like a sculpture. Like art.

The voice continued to describe, explain. The model began to cry out.

The mouth suckled and pulled away just in time for the throbbing ejaculation to be shown. Strips of white shot from the tip of the penis, semen arching, a mini-fountain on display.

Wulf wanted to whimper. Shout. Destroy something.

The denial of sexual gratification was like a barrier inside him, built inside him over time brick by brick, with fences and more fences in front of it. Overgrown. Blocked. A jungle of barricades. An army force of obstacles armed and dangerous.

He had caught himself thinking this was art. But he couldn't partake. He would not!

Now he heard himself mumbling. "Don't make me watch your pornography. I won't! This filth. This sin. I won't." He kept repeating his words again and again, louder. Until he finally demanded from the unseen cameras, "Use the collar! Use it! I don't care! I don't care!"

He shut his eyes and rose from the bed. He was afraid to leave the alcove for fear of the collar, but he paced, bumping hard into the counter.

He realized only minutes later the TV had shut off and gentle hands were helping him to stop pacing, stop banging onto the furniture.

He opened his eyes.

Locke stood by the bedside. The air had changed. No longer as sweet, but within it was the masculine scent of Locke, leafy and fresh and electric, like a lingering storm.

Wulf's mouth was so tight his teeth clenched. "Don't!" His voice sounded far away, almost a whine. "Don't touch me. Don't look at me!"

But Locke's voice kept up a kind of easy rhythm, repetitive, with sentences that mesmerized, spell-bound. "You are safe. You are protected. You are away from any strife or violence. You are safe. Steady. Easy. We will take a break now."

Chapter Eleven - Locke

Many slaves went through periods of denial and torment. But Wulf was different.

Locke watched him on the cameras and saw the splendor of him, as if he were some noble prince from a fairytale. He saw how the man inside that glorious body diminished himself, shrank away from the film on the TV, and broke himself to keep from succumbing to what he called a "sin."

Wulf pushed his own arousal down. He trapped himself. He abused himself by clamping his erection between his thighs, even pounding on it with his fisted hand.

But oh the brilliance of that body. The suppleness against rigid muscle and prominent bone, the slenderness of his physique despite the strength of sinew and brawn, all cultivating him, carving his physical form into exquisite proportions of strength and health and youth. The virility, the vital essence of maleness — all that had attracted Locke from the very beginning, longed to emerge from Wulf.

But it was all nothing — nothing so much as the look in those lost-blue eyes, the desperate anger, the danger of what a man such as Wulf fully roused in mind and body might exhibit.

A thrill went through Locke at the mere thought.

But this man was still so much a child, too. As if he had been held back in school. In life. Missing everything around him. As if he'd been bred a tool and only a tool and believed it for his culture, his country.

Wulf had lived and trained in a sheltered environment. For all of Locke's acceptance and tolerance of others, their beliefs and predilections, their addictions and preferences, he did not accept Wulf's ways, and truly believed his culture had done him no favors.

Locke was not a political expert, nor did he have such interests beyond a general knowledge, but he could not argue that Wulf's country of Rille was backward in and of itself, preaching intolerance and denying its citizens the most basic of pleasures, rewards, or even flat-out needs.

He watched from another room the misery of Wulf, the despair. That drew his attention even more. For what a prize Wulf was. And how accomplished it would feel to some day make Wulf see that for himself, within himself.

That bronzed skin of his prize was covered in sweat, though, and he shut his eyes into thin dark lines over and over, as if he were in pain. His hair grew damp at the temples and forehead, darkening. His body held a slight tremor.

What a lovely arousal, and horrible at the same time. For Wulf looked on the verge of a fight, a temper, or even tears. His toes curled. His muscles strained in his legs and arms and along his shoulders. His stomach rose and fell, matching the strain of his ribs trembling with each breath.

When Wulf began to murmur, and the murmurs grow to shouts, demanding the collar, demanding to be hurt instead of continue the lesson, Locke stopped the training session. He cut the video stream. He lowered the lights in the alcove.

Wulf did not stop his shouts.

Locke ran from the office adjacent to the training room and entered the alcove within seconds. A slave was in crisis. Peril. Locke's own training as Eminent Master took over.

First he spoke the easy calming words that worked on everyone during moments of breaking exasperation.

"You are safe. You are protected. You are away from any strife or violence. You are safe. Steady. Easy. We will take a break now."

He kept up the intonation, repeating himself.

He knew Wulf did not want to be touched, but he touched him anyway. This was medicinal. He helped him balance and regain some control of mind and body combined.

How hot that skin was. As if Wulf suffered a fever. Well, indeed he did. Unwanted arousal. The programs within all fighting for control to hold down something thought by him as the worst transgression. Sexual arousal.

The skin was like damp silk sliding against Locke's fingertips. The powerhouse of the man before him was a raging hearth of heat. Soft and hard at the same time. Raw-edged and hot. Raging and withdrawn.

Locke could not be more attracted to him than he was at this moment. His own training took over. He held himself in check.

Wulf let himself be pulled forward. His legs seemed to struggle to keep him standing beside the bed. He struggled as if he'd forgotten, for a moment, where he was.

Locke saw clearly that Wulf had lost touch with reality. Something inside him had shut down. Sex had been the catalyst.

This would not do. Not the shutting down part, and furthermore, not the fact that sex and/or sexual arousal had been the trigger. Time for Locke to remember his deeper training techniques. He could not rely on ordinary means for Wulf.

When Wulf's gaze cleared and those blue eyes brightened, Locke said, "Ah, you're back. Do I have your attention now?"

Wulf blinked. One hand reached up as if on instinct to touch his collar as he nodded.

Locke sighed at Wulf's perceived fear.

"It was your first lesson," Locke said. "I'm not going to use the collar on you for not completing your first lesson. Or even your tenth or twentieth. We are going to take this one day at a time. Your collar is there to protect you from yourself, and to protect others simply because of your short temper, your tendency toward violence… as you were taught. Not your fault. Do I make myself clear?"

"Very," Wulf said. His voice came out hoarse. "I am a dangerous person."

"Is that what you got out of my little speech?" Locke smiled to show he didn't care. It was expected. This was only Wulf's second day.

"Can you stand on your own?" Locke asked.

"Yes."

"Then let's leave here right away."

"Leave?" Wulf's pretty gaze tightened in confusion.

"Yes. We'll find a more comfortable area for you to be in. Plus, we haven't quite finished the tour of the Palace."

Wulf rocked slightly, but Locke pretended not to notice. He took up the leash, leaving a lot of slack so as not to make Wulf more nervous than he already was, and together they walked into the middle area of the long, vast room.

More slaves graced the stage at this point, naked and beautiful. Learning to comport themselves in ways to frame their physical beauty, and accent their talents.

Two males, shoulders back, heads held high, were learning to walk to accentuate their attributes. One had a plump, firm ass and he used it well as he rocked his hips, moving back and forth. The other had a large cock, and moved to show it off with pride and not shyness. He wanted to be looked at and admired for it, but he also had a lovely face, and that smile, which his master complimented, flashed white and alluring.

Two females, gorgeous as well, were a few paces away, also learning to walk with pride.

Locke loved seeing the slaves of the Palace embrace their full abilities mentally and physically to attract and keep, until old age, any owner that might be a good fit. The Palace prided itself on matching owner to slaves, on making that fit as excellent as could be. They examined everything from the tastes of all involved, to even body chemistry and the science of pheromones.

Wulf kept his gaze straight ahead.

Locke leaned into him and said, "You cannot deny their beauty. Like the statues in the garden. I know you liked those. Would you like to try it out one day? Playing statue? Not just performing art, but being art?"

Wulf glared at him and glanced down again.

Locke decided he would like to see Wulf on one of those pedestals in the garden or the front lawn one day. One day.

Locke led Wulf on a grand tour for a couple of hours. They saw the rooms for all sorts of classes, and the mall where there were stores—everything from kinky sex toys to necessities. Even clothes, which the slaves were not allowed to wear in the Palace but could wear in public outside Palace grounds. They were taught fashion to help pick out clothing for their masters' tastes. A slave learned how to shop for their master.

They stopped for a break at the mall, and a cold beverage, and a light lunch.

Naked slaves were everywhere, waiting on masters, learning trades and public behaviors. Locke had no doubt Wulf would become used to it quite quickly. It might take some time, but not too much. After a while, a new normal would set in for him. Psychologists said after three days of doing something new over and over again, humans tended to accept the new thing as their norm.

Locke thought about his bet with Malik. Malik had given him ten days to "tame" Wulf. But Locke had never thought of Wulf as untamed. Confused, maybe. Afraid. Angry, for sure.

Malik had meant, no doubt, that Locke would not be able to make a willing pleasure slave out of Wulf in ten days. Someone who might perform at will, with pride and high self-esteem. Someone who might bring the Palace a very high price.

A part of Locke had already known from the very beginning that wasn't why he'd bought Wulf. He had never been looking to make him into a pleasure slave to sell. He wanted to keep him. For pleasure, yes, but also because the man fascinated him. Had quickened him in his jaded boredom

For that reason alone, Locke had bought Wulf. Bet or no bet, Locke had already won. He owned this man. He wanted him. Ten days or ten years, it didn't matter. All in good time. He was keeping Wulf.

After lunch they went to the bathing room. Locke secured a pool for the two of them, no other intruders, and stripped down.

Wulf's eyes got very large when Locke took off all his clothes, folded them, and put them aside.

Locke had a great body. No shame there. Lean, with fine hard muscles, and sun-toasted skin, for he spent his summers at the outdoor pools at least an hour a day swimming and reading.

He jutted his hips forward to see if Wulf might notice. Nothing.

Locke kept his grin to himself. His cock was nice. But he couldn't expect it to interest everybody. But with time, he hoped for just that where Wulf was concerned. Interest. Curiosity. Attraction. More? He dared to hope. But not because he was the best at what he did. Not because he was a master. This was different. This was something he wanted, someone he desired all on his own. For himself.

He could have sex with any slave he wanted, any time he wanted. All Palace slaves were open to him in that way. He was an Eminent Master. He could take over any slave's training at any time without question. But it was Wulf he wanted.

That had never happened to him before.

This new feeling was like a poet falling in love with a poem. Or something similar. He couldn't figure it out, but he didn't need to. It was what it was. Not about a bet. Not about an altruistic rescue of some hopeless soul.

Droplets of warm water hit his legs, interrupting his thoughts.

Wulf slid into the pool. The bubbles swirled about his chest, the water giving his skin a glow. The wake of his weight in the pool sent a spray up toward Locke.

Locke stepped onto the top shelf of the pool. As he bent to take his seat in the roiling liquid, Wulf ignored him. Locke watched him let himself slide slowly under the water. He came up seconds later, shaking his wet hair back.

If Locke hadn't known better, he would have thought the man was putting on a show for him. Seducing him with the action of lifting his muscular arms and pushing his hair flat on his head.

But Wulf was in his own world, unconscious of his affect on anyone or anything around him. The water slid down his bronze arms in rainy lines, glistening. It dripped in little falls from clumps of his hair until there were only quivering droplets left to tease the ends.

Wulf's eyes closed, but not too tight like before in the alcove in front of the TV. This time the muscles of his face relaxed. His lashes barely dusted the tops of his cheeks.

Locke watched as Wulf leaned back against the ledge, lowering his arms and trailing his hands across the pool's surface. He was clearly enjoying this part of his training: learning how to relax. Locke made sure the fact that this, too, was a lesson remained a secret, or Wulf would not have understood. He would have tensed. He would have endured, not enjoyed. Now, watching Wulf let go for a few moments was nice.

Some green ferns in pots draped alongside the pool, giving Wulf and Locke a little more privacy here than they would ordinarily have. They gave off a fresh, healthy scent. The water itself had a slight chlorine smell, but not overwhelming.

Locke turned to Wulf, who was still glistening, blinking the water from his eyelashes. "Do you like to swim?"

"It's fine," came the low response.

Locke said, "Good. We can make swimming part of our daily routine, then finish off here in the hot pools."

"Whatever."

But Locke could tell by Wulf's tone and the way his muscles relaxed in his shoulders that Wulf would enjoy the swimming routine. That it was something he could wrap his mind around instead of lessons in such dreaded things as pleasure, manners and how to be a good slave.

Together, they sat in silence, letting the bubbles do their work.

The liquid warmth caressed Locke's body until he almost fell asleep. He had been working hard the last couple of years and rarely took time for himself other than short breaks for exercise and swimming. These next ten days were for him and him alone. He had taken the time off from his Palace job to attend to his slave, and to take on Malik's challenge.

This bit about relaxing, he realized, was a lesson not only for Wulf. Locke needed it. He really should be taking better care of himself now that he was no longer a twenty-something upstart.

He spent far too much time at a desk doing paperwork. He went to the auctions with Malik to get out, but it hadn't been enough. Until Wulf appeared. Until Wulf turned his world upside-down during a simple fall off an auction stage, and a brief touch when Locke had caught his hard, beautiful form in his arms.

Locke pretended to mind his own business and allow Wulf time to soak, but in truth he kept a peripheral eye on him the whole time they were in the pool.

Finally, when Locke's fingers began to wrinkle, and he began to feel a little too warm, he stood.

"All right." Locke kept his voice low. "Time to dry off. I'm taking you through the sculpture gardens next."

Wulf did not react.

Locke ignored the lack of response and stepped naked out of the pool. A helpful young, naked slave ran toward him, bringing a stack of clean towels and bowing deeply.

Slowly, Locke dried himself off, first his legs, then his back and chest. Lastly, he ruffled the towel over his hair.

His clothing lay in a neatly folded pile on a bench nearby. With a slight turn of his head, he observed Wulf, who was finally moving forward in the water, little wavelets streaming alongside his hips as he float-walked to the pool's shallow steps.

Locke went to the bench, hearing the water shift and churn as Wulf's large body left the pool. He grabbed his pants and stepped into them, pulling them up quickly and fastening them. He grabbed his shirt and turned.

Wulf was standing naked and wet by the tiled edge. His hair made pretty, shining clumps about his handsome face. His muscles gleamed, sleek beneath damp skin. His buttocks were tightly drawn inward, and there was a lovely concave sculptured look to the side of his upper thigh where it met the hip bone.

Wulf should be in paintings. Wulf, he thought, should be a sculpture in the garden—nothing short of the main, central attraction, for all other slaves paled in comparison to this man's natural, innocent but strong beauty.

Chapter Twelve – Wulf

Wulf had not wanted to leave the hot spring—or pool, or whatever it was called. It had been the best part of his day so far. He had been able to relax for the first time since being captured by the enemy. Even his sleep had been fraught with tensions.

The pool provided a strange, meditative release. It soothed like nothing else had in his life so far.

After he'd dried himself, and Locke had dressed, Locke led Wulf to a pair of doors with bright, paned windows. The sun came in through them in white sheets, almost glaring. The doors opened onto a veranda with a brick path edged by plants and trees.

The air was cool but not too cold. Everything smelled of newly turned earth, sweet blooms, and crumbling clay from old pots that held ivy, orchids, and ferns.

As they walked beneath the large trees, the shadows of leaves and branches dappled the pathway. The pool and then this. Wulf allowed himself to remain relaxed.

Beside him, Locke's presence was like a firm, steady force. It promised safety, even fairness. He did not feel in danger. Nor had he felt any danger from the pool where the master had stripped naked and shown himself off to Wulf for the first time.

Wulf had had some trouble thinking, breathing, even swallowing at first. His master was a handsome man with the dark coloring he preferred in his fantasies. His body, trim and toned, had less musculature than Wulf's, and was more angular, more chiseled. To think of it made Wulf feel a tremble inside as if a cool breeze had blown against the short hairs of his arms and legs.

The bricks beneath Wulf's feet scraped lightly. Locke led him beyond the trees to a park-like area, much like the front of the Palace, with lots of grass, oaks, and small bushes.

Scattered throughout the grassy hillocks and dips, marble pedestals dotted the landscape. Upon them were beautiful statues of shapes and sizes and colorings. For a moment, as he had upon his arrival at the Palace, Wulf did think they really were statues.

As they came closer to the first, Wulf saw it was a live human being under all that paint. The man held a pose with one arm raised, the other curved behind him, and one foot forward. He looked like an ancient god straight from Olympus, painted in gold and silver brushstrokes all over his naked body.

Wulf could see the man's chest rise and fall with each breath. He shimmered like metal or polished stone, but quivered like a living being, warm and vital with blood running through his veins. Even his hair was dyed a stiff gold color, but wisps of it quivered in the breeze.

For a moment, the beauty encapsulated Wulf. And he forgot where he was. He had denied these statues at first. Had hated the thought of them. Now he wondered what it might be like to be standing there, covered in paint, proudly posing for the trees, the sky and all who might walk by.

Wulf's head spun.

"You like him?" Locke asked, breaking the reverie.

He could not admit it, and shook his head, glancing away from the sight.

"Come along, there are so many more, each one more beautiful than the last. This art is a beautiful design toward physical and mental discipline. It is both calming and freeing, to know such control."

"That doesn't make sense."

"No?"

"You contradict yourself when you say it's freeing and controlling when you talk of discipline and freedom in the same sentence."

Locke simply tilted his head and smiled.

"Well," Wulf said, moving toward another pedestal, "it makes no sense."

This time when he looked up he saw two humans intertwined, a male and a female embraced, all in silver with black, straight hair flowing behind both their bodies, braided together.

Wulf swallowed hard. He had no words. They were lovely. He could only blink and stare, then force himself to look away.

The next statues were even more erotic. He may have stared longer at the two men together than he meant to. One knelt before the other. The standing man had a full erection. How he kept his organ hard while remaining so still, while doing nothing but looking straight ahead at the hill beyond the Palace, Wulf could not know. The kneeling man had his head poised and lips pursed right in front of that hard cock, as if he were about to kiss it but had been frozen in time before reaching his destination.

That was discipline! But freeing? Body and mind could betray each other at a moment's notice. But this man held his pose, and there was a fierceness in his dark eyes that rivaled that of even the strongest warriors Wulf had served with.

Locke began to move on down the line of sculptures, but Wulf lingered.

Locke stopped and turned back to him. "We can come here every day to see the new ones," he said. "If you'd like."

Wulf turned his head to the side. How could he admit he would like that very much without showing weakness? He took a deep breath, held it. One more glance at the two men. It couldn't hurt.

When he looked back at them, their pose had change just a little. The standing man's eyes had moved and were now looking at Wulf. The kneeling man had opened his pursed mouth and the tip of a pink tongue could be seen.

These two were so utterly masculine, their bodies like waves and curving promises of held back power.

Ripples of heat attacked Wulf's skin. A flutter of warmth settled in his balls.

He frowned.

"It's all right to be moved by their art. These two have worked hard to maintain this pose. They can go for at least an hour now. When they started, they could not hold position for more than five minutes."

"Maybe they are fierce and this art opens their strengths."

"Yes, maybe." Locke smiled.

When they finished their tour, Wulf returned to the inner Palace with a strange sort of fulfillment in his chest. He couldn't explain it. His first full day here, and already he was succumbing?

But there was such beauty surrounding him, if he allowed himself to see it. This was his life now. He had nothing else. He'd always been good at adapting and obeying in his former life. But only to those who had authority over him.

He did not recognize this foreign country yet has having authority. Not in his heart. But Locke, well, Locke had bought him. Wulf belonged to him now. He could understand that, even if he didn't like it, or agree with the law of legalized pleasure slavery.

And he was coming to realize, Locke wasn't so bad.

So far.

*

Over the next few days, dinner was served every night in Wulf's room, with the brightly lit skyline for their view.

Locke ate with him now, instead of just watching him. They had fresh seafood, steak or grilled chicken on beds of rice. Green salads. Ice cream. Foods Wulf was not used to.

He'd eaten so many bagged meals, so much stale bread and wilted greens. He was not used to such fantastic cooking. And such gleaming plates and glasses of wine and golden cutlery. No more paper plates and pre-cooked meals in plastic bags. No more military mess halls with plastic divided trays and liquid slop called stew — more like soup — for most meals.

Every morning, Locke made good on his promise. They went to the pool and swam for half an hour, then soaked in the hot pools until their fingers were wrinkled.

They took long walks in the sculpture gardens.

It amazed Wulf that in all that time, Locke had never tried to touch him sexually. Yes, he had tried to show him sexual images, and help him open his mind to the idea that pleasure was not the sin he had been taught it was. But Locke the master — the training master — remained apart. Maybe even a bit aloof.

It did not unnerve Wulf. It made him feel vindicated. At first.

But the fourth day came the same as the rest, and Wulf began to wonder. If his master was trying to be friends with him, then demand the pleasures he was required to teach Wulf, that would be worse.

Wulf could never be friends with him. Not with someone who called himself an Eminent Master. Not with someone who trained sex slaves day in and day out. A person like that had to have no soul. Even if he pretended to.

No, friendship could never be allowed.

The thought made Wulf anxious. At breakfast, he barely touched his food.

Locke, always kind in tone, asked, "Not hungry?"

Wulf shook his head. They were sitting at the booth where they had eaten their first breakfast. Wulf stared at the scar on the wall where he'd made a hole, yanking his leash as he had lunged for Locke.

The hole had been repaired, but a slight dent and discoloration remained. The scar. His mark. What he would leave behind here if he ever got away. *Ever* translated to *never*.

Wulf had become imprisoned for life.

Locke said, "Even though it is October, the day is very warm as tends to happen here in the south. I thought we'd use the outdoor pool for our swim."

Wulf lowered his head until his chin almost touched his bare chest.

"We can relax in the sun for a while," Locke added.

"Why?" Now Wulf looked up, saw those dark eyes that should have been beady and cold — and maybe they were in his worst nightmares — but were really quite warm with lively golden flecks in the irises.

"What?"

"Why bother?" Wulf huffed.

Locke's gaze turned inward, then, and Wulf watched his face go placid as his mind began to work the puzzle, something it seemed Locke was very good at, like his name, unlocking the riddle, or locking it up so only he could see and admire it.

"There are environments here designed to ease your stress. This is one of them. That is why we bother."

Locke's answer, patient as always, never failed to be correct and calm.

"Those are tricks, then."

Locke's brows came together, not quite frowning, but obviously not happy with the direction of the conversation, either. "If it is a trick to make you comfortable, then you may be wrong in thinking that."

Wulf tried not to pout. He forced his muscles to remain slack. But he felt hot quite suddenly. The towel beneath his naked ass felt slightly damp.

"After our swim, I thought maybe you'd like to see the sculpture garden at the front of the grounds."

"Because you think I like them."

"I know you like them. Maybe you secretly want to be one of them."

For a moment, Wulf wanted to lunge forward, as he had on his first day. A purely aggressive response to the building anger inside him. Anger for no reason, really, except that he was frustrated and he didn't know why.

He suppressed it. Maybe the collar had worked in that regard, but either way, there was no use to fight Locke and always lose in addition to going through the pain of a shock collar set on "high."

It seemed he was succumbing. And it wasn't just the collar controlling him. He was forgetting his position as a warrior too often. And his firm beliefs of what constituted good, and what was evil. It was Locke's doing, he knew. Locke was getting under his skin. Controlling him. Wulf needed to gain back some control.

"I don't want any of it. Or any of this. The Palace. You. Don't you understand that by now?" His chest felt constricted. Weak. He was so weak. It wasn't right.

Locke took a breath. He did not answer.

"Take me to the training room." Wulf's own request surprised him, but he needed to do something to distance himself from Locke, to erase whatever friendly connection might be forming between them. It was the only way.

One eyebrow rose in response.

"Well," Wulf said, "I'm going to end up there anyway. Why prolong it? Do you think you can coddle and tempt me to want to go there? It will be no different a week from now, a month, a year. I don't want any of it. And placating me with swimming and hot tubs and grand tours and meals is insulting! So we might as well get the real training over with."

"I see. So. You are calling the shots."

"What?"

"I am the master here. I give you orders. Correct?"

Wulf glowered.

"What you appear to like — enjoy, perhaps — is part of my process in deciding what comes next in our relationship, and your training."

"Relationship?"

"Yes. The one between owner and slave. It is a relationship, whether you like that word or not."

Wulf did not like it. Not at all. His lungs shook a little, but he inhaled deeper to feel a sharpness there where he held back his rage, forcing himself to not give over to emotions, or show weakness of any sort.

"We go back to the training room when I say we go back to the training room, understand?" Locke said quietly.

"I want to go now!" His voice came out louder than he'd intended. A few people at nearby tables, slaves and masters alike, raised their heads and glanced at them.

"I think we are done here," Locke said. He folded his napkin, placed it at the center of the tables, and stood. He reached out and took the end of Wulf's leash in his grip, something he hadn't done in two days.

Wulf stood. After his outburst, although everyone had gone back to their food, he still felt as if they were all staring. At him. Feeling more exposed and naked than ever, he pinched his lips, stuck his chin out, and followed Locke out of the dining hall.

For the first few steps, he couldn't see. Not tears, but rage made him blind, though he blinked back sudden dampness he would never admit to.

The collar bound him tight against his throat. He hadn't noticed it the last couple of days. And that was another sign of his weakness. Had he gotten used to it so quickly? He needed to feel that collar. And remain aware of everything else that was happening around him. And that rage inside him. How could he have forgotten that?

The answer: Locke had plied him with everything Wulf showed an interest in. He loved to swim. Locke was also correct about the art; Wulf loved the gardens, the sculptures, the beautiful live art that was unlike anything so grand he had ever seen. That people could make that out of their own bodies amazed him. That art had never seemed pornographic to him. Not quite a sin as he at first tried to tell himself. They were too beautiful, too still and serene to be a sin. He thought of them as majestic. Noble. Even dignified.

Locke was tricking him with these things. Wulf needed to remember that.

Wulf stumbled as Locke turned down a corridor different from all the ones they been down before.

Panic made his chest send shooting pains into his stomach and shoulders. He saw the leash go taut. Saw Locke turn slowly, giving a slight yank as the collar tugged against the back of Wulf's neck.

Both Locke's eyebrows shot up high on his forehead probably because he didn't expect Wulf to fall.

Wulf felt his mouth open. He put up his hands to brace against the air as if he could stop his fall, as if he could stop the impending pain. He heard his own inhale like a rush of wind foretelling a coming storm. Staccato-like, rattling.

His knees slammed against the tile floor. Then—nothing. No collar pain. No shock.

Wulf's hair swung to the sides of his face, a golden curtain closing, opening, closing. His breath came out in a whoosh.

He looked in front of him from where he now knelt to see a pair of black-clad legs. Tilting his head back, Wulf saw Locke standing calmly beside him, looking down with those so dark but so kind eyes, the muscles around them slightly bunched.

"Hmm," Locke said. "I must have forgotten to turn it on."

Wulf's jaw went slack. He could kill Locke. Right now. No one would stop him. He wouldn't get away with it, but he could accomplish that much.

But Wulf did not make any move toward that despite the voices in his mind shouting in irate tones. He continued to kneel before Locke. Before that bleak, dark presence that never seemed fazed. Or hurried. Or worried.

Locke's plush pink lips parted. "Did you panic when the leash went taut?"

Wulf's gaze misted, but he did not look away.

"Did you slip?"

Finally Wulf answered. "I was not paying attention when you turned."

"Mind on the training room you so want to go to, eh?" Locke asked.

Much to his humiliation, Wulf's face heated. He knew Locke saw it, how his face must be so pink now, darkening with all his emotions exposed.

All this, Locke and his calmness and his questions. A trick.

Using all his strength to ignore his burning embarrassment, Wulf said, "Why would you turn my collar off?"

Locke's lips turned up, almost a smile but not. "It must have been one of the times we were in the pool. It's not such a good combination in water. I turn it off every time we go swimming and into the hot pools. I simply forgot to turn it back on."

The last time they had gone swimming was yesterday morning. Wulf's collar had been inert for twenty-four hours? He could not believe it.

"It didn't seem to matter. It doesn't now. Or does it?" Locke asked. Always enigmatic, always so fucking calm.

Wulf didn't want to think about it, but he couldn't help himself. He realized things had gotten very complicated in only a few days. He did not want to kill Locke, but he wanted to want to kill him. He wanted to hate this place and its sculpture gardens and placid people, but what he wanted, and how his mind and body reacted were in conflict.

In so short a time, he had fallen so far. Had he always been so weak?

Locke held out a hand, facing up.

Wulf did not take it. He pushed down to the floor with one palm and stood up, perfectly balanced, all in order, body at least, if not quite his mind.

"Well?" Locke asked.

Wulf knew what he was asking. "You do not have to turn the collar back on. I won't attack you." It sounded inane. Of course Locke would not believe him, and he would not get that wish.

"Well, maybe I'll reduce it to low then," Locke said.

Wulf blinked at him. He couldn't ask for worse. He wanted to. He wanted to be able to take it, take on any torture this place wanted to mete out to him. Instead, he nodded. "Low is fine."

"Good." Locke smile and turned, leash in hand, slack.

Outraged at himself, Wulf followed.

Chapter Thirteen – Locke

Locke watched Wulf try not to enjoy himself too much in the fresh water of the outdoor pool. But Wulf was liking it almost too much.

White-striped sunlight patterned the patio in front of the pool. Locke had finished his laps and lay on a lounge chair soaking up the warmth of the day.

Wulf always swam longer and harder than Locke. His youth and pent-up energy needed to vent somewhere. For all his protests, he had been the first one in the water and the last one out.

The clean chlorinated water scented the air along with a faint perfume of fall accompanied by leaves on the wind and dusty breezes. Small white clouds scudded across a fairytale blue sky.

Wulf pulled himself from the water and Locke could not take his eyes off him. His arms bulged. He came up like a merman from the sparkling depths, water rolling over his hair and down his sides, chest and legs as he lifted himself to his thighs, up and over the lip of the pool, then to his knees and quickly stood.

Still shy, he turned away from Locke, shaking his mane of hair which, when wet, looked like sheets of wavering brown honey. He grabbed a towel, dried himself cursorily, and laid it on a lounge chair two lounges away from Locke.

Normally, Locke insisted Wulf remain close to him at all times. Wulf obeyed without having to be reminded. But today was different. Things had changed. Wulf had learned new things about himself. It always happened with slaves. Anger. Depression. And denial. Not always in the same order. But all happened before they accepted their new lives. Some took longer than others, but they all went through it.

Wulf was a more difficult case, but he would get through it, too. Locke had infinite patience, but where Wulf was concerned, he wished it was quicker. The man infatuated him to the point of obsession. Even when apart, Locke couldn't stop looking at him through cameras day and night. He paced himself, but it proved more difficult than he'd anticipated.

Wulf lay back, hands crossed over his groin. A typical pose. Modest. Inhibited. But also wise in protecting the genitals from sunburn.

Locke held back his smile. He wanted to smile a lot these days. Wulf, despite his offended manner and protesting glares, stimulated him. It wasn't simple physical attraction, though that was the initial draw. It was mental as well. Wulf was a prize, someone with conviction, technically not a criminal, either. He was a prisoner. But he had been an upstanding citizen... simply in the wrong country.

War brought down casualties. Wulf was one of them.

After half an hour baking in the southern sunlight, Locke took Wulf, despite his dissenting stare, to the front of the massive estate to tour the sculptures by the Palace entry way.

Wulf said nothing, but did a lot of reproachful breathing. But as Locke watched him, he saw Wulf could not help but look.

More than looking at the sculptures, Wulf gazed at them for long minutes, his face taking on a state of grace. He would have denied it if Locke had told him this in so many words. Locke could have shown him video of his rapt expression, and Wulf would probably still deny, insisting Locke read him wrong.

Singles. Couples. Groups. Some of the sculptures out in front of the Palace were massive displays of feasts, operas, dances and orgies, all frozen, all made of live bodies eager to present themselves as art.

When Wulf approached them, many of the sculpture's eyes moved to look upon him, as if gazing back at yet another work of art. If Wulf noticed, he did not react. He merely gazed. His muscles twitched.

It was during these times that Wulf seemed to forget his outrage, his new status, his nudity. He became more himself, more the man Locke wanted to know.

That night, at dinner, Wulf said, "I am making no progress. Nothing matters. Tomorrow, I ask you to take me to back to the training room. Do you what you need to do to me. Force me to obey, or whatever. I'm tired of you pretending to show me any of this means anything more than it is, non-consensual sexual gratification for the wealthy and privileged."

"Well, yes it is about sexual gratification mostly for the wealthy and privileged. But not non-consensual, since every slave signs a consent form."

"I didn't."

"I know that."

Wulf was silent for a moment. Then he said, "Is that why you haven't touched me?"

Not answering his question directly, Locke said, "Things went a little wrong when I took you to the training room that first day. I will decide when you go back."

"It doesn't matter. You'll do what you need to do to turn me into a perfect slave."

"Perhaps."

Wulf let out a quick breath, set his tray aside and stood. "I'm tired."

"It's early."

"I want to go to bed."

Locke watched him move to the bathroom as if to shower. Or brush his teeth.

How badly Wulf seemed to want to control the things he no longer could. He might have made a very good master. But that would never ever happen for him. Not in Avilan.

Locke decided it would benefit both of them to turn in early.

Standing at the bathroom door threshold, looking at the offended look on Wulf's face as he put down his toothbrush, Locke said, "I will allow us both extra sleep this one evening."

"And tomorrow?"

"Tomorrow we will see if you are ready for the training room. Maybe. Maybe not."

"I don't care anymore," Wulf said, staring down at the sink.

"Yes, it must seem that way. I know."

"You think you know me?" Wulf almost whispered.

"More than you think," Locke said. "More than you think."

Wulf's eyebrows came together, creasing the skin above his nose but never managing to mar his beautiful complexion, or his handsome visage.

Locke turned away. He needed to do something else this evening to take his mind off Wulf. It was getting to be an obsession.

He was on leave, a vacation, but that didn't mean his stacks of paperwork went away. He decided he would use the extra evening hours to tackle them.

*

Malik came toward Locke on the upper level hallway leading to the wing of master apartments.

"Locke! Where's your ever-present golden shadow? Giving up early for the night?"

"My paperwork is piling up. Besides, Wulf needed the break."

"I thought you were on vacation. Giving in to him, then, I see." Malik's grin widened. "Worried about our bet?"

"Not in the least."

"Well, then, how is he? In bed, I mean."

Locke lowered his eyelids and looked at Malik through his lashes, wondering if he'd heard this impertinent tone from Malik all these years but was only noticing it now.

"You'll never know."

"But for our bet, I'll have to know the details. I'll have to see how he performs, of course."

"He will perform when and how I tell him to. And not for you. I own him, remember? He's mine."

Malik, still smiling as if he hadn't a care in the world, said, "A tad territorial, aren't you? I like it. I haven't seen this side of you before."

"The bet was about taming him, not bedding him." Locke stared into Malik's face, trying to see something deeper in him, and failing. He'd called Malik his best friend, but somehow this bet had changed things.

"Oh, and now you're defending him. Splendid! I love it. I could see at the auction that this one affected you. I wasn't sure how deeply, but now — now I see. It's wonderful."

Locke frowned; Malik's tone made everything less a compliment and more a joke. In the past, he'd taken a word such as "wonderful" as a compliment, but not today. Not this evening.

"Well," Locke said, turning away. "I'm off for the night."

"Yes, and good night to you, too." Malik took a step back. Stopped. "Oh, one more thing. Uh... the bet was about a ten day makeover — into a pleasure slave. With you, Eminent Master, as his trainer. That was the bet. Just saying, you lose if he doesn't perform."

Locke froze in mid-step. Turned. He took a deep breath. They'd been friends for a long time, and Malik was often glib, clever and ridiculous — a fun guy most of the time. But now Locke stared at him with a sudden realization that Malik was the type who enjoyed others' discomfort.

He was a bit of a sadist, and many excellent masters had traits of sadism which made them good at their jobs. But

Malik, he now realized, had made his friendly bet when they were both drinking, trying to alleviate their stale jadedness in attending up to a hundred slave auctions a year.

That he could obviously see Locke had a fondness for his new slave, it appeared to give him all the more pleasure to see that cause him to lose the bet. That was not the desired behavior of a friend.

Or, Locke chastised himself, maybe he was being too sensitive. His feelings, lately, had been all over the place.

Locke said, jaw stiff, "Do you think the bet is what I even care about?"

Malik revealed white teeth as he gave an exaggerated shrug. "I don't know, do you?"

"No, Malik. I'll be clear. I could give a shit about the bet."

Malik laughed, and Locke's quick mind began to redefine Malik's character from one moment to the next.

"We'll see," Malik said.

As Locke walked away, he wondered why he had suddenly felt so furious. Malik was not the enemy. He'd known him for years. They'd gotten along fine. They'd even trained slaves together. They both had very different techniques to get their jobs done. Malik was the more physical one, Locke the more cerebral. But that had never seemed to matter.

As Locke turned down the corridor that led to his suite, he thought about Wulf again.

When was he *not* thinking of him? But more specifically, he focused on Wulf's behavior, how he'd hit that second wall that came upon all slaves after they breeched the anger-wall. Depression. Or maybe it was denial. The two reactions in humans were connected.

Humans pretended not to care because caring and losing hurt too much. And then there was the hurt, the pain of knowing your previous life was over, shut away. The saying: *You can never go home again* was literal for slaves. They started new lives. They became, at worst, objects, things, and at best, companions for masters the Palace paired them with in the outside world once they were ready to be sold. If owners and slaves fell in love with one another after the sale—even better. But no matter what happened to a slave after they signed their consent forms, their lives did indeed start over. For better or worse, it was a new beginning.

Wulf had asked for the training room, which he hated, because he wanted to get it all over with. He didn't want to feel. He had not liked any idea that Locke might be trying to get to know him or befriend him. And Locke could not blame him.

Wulf was different. As a One-Night Thrall, he had been labeled dangerous. And then there had been no consent. That fact alone stacked the odds against Locke as a trainer, and against Wulf as a man who had been thrust into an alien nightmare.

Locke's body quickened as he thought of Wulf's more unique and special obstacles in facing a new life. He liked that about Wulf, that he wasn't like everyone else. Wulf was powerful and without guilt. He had truly committed no crime. He was a captured enemy. That all by itself was rather alluring.

If for no other reason, Locke wanted him on that count. Wulf was a force to face down. An equal. He'd not waited for an order to return to the training room. He'd asked for it, figuring out how to take power back into his own hands. How Locke loved him for that challenging personality.

The beauty, as irresistible as it was, only complimented that higher spirit, that fighting will in Wulf.

He'd used the word *magnificent* to describe him so many times already, and he would use it again. For this man was a feat of nature that went uncontested in Locke's mind.

He almost turned away from the door of his suite to head back to his office. He wanted to spend more hours watching his slave, as he had every night.

But, no. Tonight he would try to back off. Reclaim some of his own strong demeanor which Wulf's presence leached more of every day.

He would get some paperwork done, and he swore to himself to avoid the lesser surveillance on his own suite computer.

Tonight he would be a master only. An Eminent Master. He would do his job, get some paperwork done. He would distance himself from both his personal feelings and his new acquisition's feelings.

Tomorrow was another day.

Chapter Fourteen – Wulf

Into the night, distant lights flickered in a city unknown, beyond a wide window and below the park of the Palace, down the grassy hill past great, concrete walls and iron gates, lights and more lights glimmered and glared, everything big and small at once. *Everything* was beyond Wulf's reach, displacing him in time and space.

In the glass, his dim reflection greeted him. All he was had been reduced to this, a silhouette upon cold panes. An unclothed man alone with nothing to call his own.

The room smelled of flowers from the body wash he'd used in the shower. He took showers often. Trying to get clean. He could not forget the torment of the touches in the warehouse and at the auction. The indignity. The degradation. And in the military, when in the field, showers had been a luxury almost unheard of.

Though he had not yet been abused at the Palace, Wulf's state, naked and facing a life of depravity, made his body feel different, not his own, a costume he could not escape.

It bothered him — had all day — that Locke would not take him to the training room now that he had asked. He was agreeing to go! Was that not enough?

But while Locke allowed him to choose his own meals most of the times, he was onto him about this. He would not allow Wulf to make any of the bigger decisions about his fate.

Wulf wanted to lose his mind, get through the actions and motions required of using his body as a sex tool. If he faced all that, he could put his fears to rest and never have to make decisions about it again. And maybe, just maybe he could seduce his way out of his predicament.

Thinking about sex — when it would happen, how it would be — was too hard. It was getting him into trouble. He had to be with Locke all day long, feel his dark-clad, strangely warm presence nearby. See him as he slid naked into pools, hear him as he spoke in his bass timbre that set Wulf's bones rattling, and wakened a weird, hot flame just below his navel.

If that wasn't bad enough, when Locke left him each evening, Wulf could not get the man out of his thoughts. He thought of him while bathing, while shaving, while trying to sleep. Locke's face would soar about his thoughts, offering a strength of command that Wulf's body inadvertently responded to, and an unwavering source of power that eclipsed all else, including the looming personality of the Palace itself.

It was conditioning, Wulf told himself. Stockholm Syndrome. He was forced to rely on the master for all his needs, so he looked to him for everything else beyond that.

It was that and nothing else. It had to be. Locke was an expert. He gave Wulf the illusion of having some choice in things like meals and even this evening tonight off, but it was still a sham.

Wulf wasn't ignorant. He could see a bigger picture. He'd been forced into roles his whole life by a culture that demanded from him a service that involved violence and war. He'd accepted that with grace. He'd been told all his life it was the right thing to do.

Now the players had changed, and the culture. The uniforms and rules might differ, but they were still uniforms and rules. If he was smart enough to see this, why should he be surprised that one life led to another involving extremes of lapsed freedoms?

He'd seen something in Locke's eyes that told him Locke had similar thoughts.

He glanced up and around the room. He knew cameras were everywhere. Was Locke watching him even now?

He sighed aloud, the room echoing his breath, the air stilling again. Whatever the reason, the man Locke would not leave his thoughts. And the small stone of heat lodged in his abdomen would not cool.

*

The room was dark, but the lights from the city spilled their glitter onto the tables and chairs, and left jagged shadows on Wulf's bed.

Something felt different. Wulf's senses flared. He sat up, the blanket sliding down his chest.

"Ah," said a voice, and a clicking sound came from Wulf's right. A tiny orange light burst upon the shadows.

A male silhouette all in black stood about six feet away from his bed staring him. He lifted the flame to his lips, lit a cigarette, and the flame went out. A dot of thinner orange light poked the air.

Wulf heard a puff of breath and smelled tobacco.

"Wulf is your name, yes? Such a strong and powerful name. And now you are awake," said the silhouette.

Not Locke. Someone else. A stranger.

Wulf's instincts tightened his muscles. The hairs on his body stood up. He was not frightened at first, for he had no trouble defending himself physically.

But the collar shifted on his neck, reminding him of the constant ache of it, as well as its purpose. If Locke hadn't turned it back on…

He could not know for sure. Or if Locke had engaged the collar, was it on low as he had promised Wulf? Even a low charge would hurt. He had no experience with it, no experience of the lesser pain, only that to risk any episode with the collar sent his blood racing in terror.

The collar left him nothing. It virtually emasculated him.

Fear threatened. He could only hope that maybe Locke would be watching even now in the middle of the night.

"Wulf, I can feel your tension from here."

"Who are you?"

"My name is Malik."

"What are you doing here?"

"I can go wherever I wish. I am a master."

Smoke curled into Wulf's nostrils. He could not see the essence, but the cloying scent was strong.

"You are not my master."

"No." There was a hint of laughter in that response.

"It is the middle of the night. Locke does not allow anyone in here past eleven." Wulf saw the time on a clock by the bed, but automatically reached for his phone. He could call Locke. He never had, but the phone was there to reach him if necessary.

"Oh?" Footsteps. "I wouldn't do that if I were you. I have control of your collar."

Wulf dropped the phone. It landed on the top of the blanket by his thigh.

Now the man — Malik — stood by the bedside, knocking his knees against the mattress.

"No need to call him."

"Who?"

"Your master." This time, laughter whispered in the dark. "Locke and I are old friends. Perhaps you remember me from the auction? When we both saw you, oh my. Finally! A little excitement to an otherwise rather dreary day. A One-Night Thrall! And what a specimen of male virility, a masculine treat for the eye. Locke is drawn to the male form much more so than I. I knew he had to have you. He needed a challenge. Well, fuck, we both did. So I made him a bet."

"A bet?"

"Oh yes, a friendly bet, is all. With money involved, of course. I told him if he bought you he would not be able to tame you. I gave him ten days. It's not enough time for anyone to be fully trained, you see, but Locke was mesmerized and oh how he surprised me when he took the bet. Me? I think it's rather impossible to tame someone like you. You'd need restraints first and foremost and I can see right now he hasn't even gotten to that part and we're half-way through the bet. I've read your file. You haven't even consented to this. But Locke, well, he's a good-natured guy, and smitten. And too proud to say no to the likes of me."

Wulf blinked, trying to take it all in. Malik supplied a lot of information quite quickly. But the worst was how he talked about Locke, not like a friend but like everything for them was a joke. And as if he thought Locke was flawed in some irritating way. Locke did not seem that shallow to Wulf at all.

And here he was defending him in his own mind.

"I—I don't understand why you're here. In my room," Wulf said slowly. His bed shifted as Malik hit the side again with his knees.

"Just checking up. The bet is for a lot of money. I wanted to see you for myself."

"In the middle of the night." It was not a question.

"Why yes. What better time than to find you alone and with all your defenses down?"

The smoke from the master's cigarette curled up Wulf's nose and down his throat. He suppressed a cough. He'd never smoked, though some of his comrades had. Still, he'd never gotten used to the smell.

Before Wulf could respond further, Malik said in a drawling tone, "So, tell me your thoughts, your desires, your deepest dreams, my handsome Wulf."

"Wh-what?"

"Has no one ever asked you that before?"

"Could you just—leave?"

"Oh, I'm afraid it doesn't work that way, my boy. I'm the master here." Another laugh. "Just so there's no confusion, and I'm sure Locke has made it clear to you, you don't get to tell anyone else what to do. You obey orders."

Wulf sat very still with his palms flat against his thighs on top of the covers. He glanced at his phone only inches away. But the collar pressed against the sides of his neck reminded him he was told by a master not to touch it.

He thought very hard about what any other slave in his predicament might do. Offer themselves, of course. That was how they were trained. To willingly submit to any master who asked it of them. Those were the rules. But those slaves were Palace slaves, not yet owned by any single master.

Wulf was Locke's. He was already owned. What were the rules if you belonged to someone? If you were theirs and theirs alone? If he was Locke's property, then did he have to obey Malik?

"Well, you haven't answered me yet, slave," Malik said.

"About what?"

"Ah, dreams and desires, those elusive phantoms that make up a life, or at the very least, a fantasy life."

Wulf stayed silent.

"Have you none?" the master asked.

"I belong to Locke. That is my life."

"So it would seem, but I'm afraid, my boy, it is only temporary. The bet ends in five days. You are nobody, not even a consenting slave. You were slated for death days ago. When Locke loses the bet, you'll be sold. Your original file will show you are a One-Night Thrall. It will be a death camp for you, no doubt about it."

Days ago, Wulf had not cared. He'd wanted to die. He might even have begged for it. Though he did not want to be at the Palace, he'd changed somewhat, for deep inside he did want to live. Maybe he always had. And Locke had assured him he would not be killed. He'd believe him. But now, how could this be? A bet? For money? Was this all any of this was for Locke?

"So before all that horrible dying stuff, wouldn't it be nice to share a dream or two? I'm here. I'm listening."

This was not a friendly chat. Wulf heard the cruelty dripping from he words even as Malik kept his voice light and teasing.

In the war, Wulf had not allowed himself too many dreams. He only wanted to get through the day alive. And he wanted to be proper, and seen as proper. That was it. He read a lot, but did not ever wish himself to be those characters in the books. Only to get through his day, every day.

Now, it was strange. Malik spoke of dreams and desires and after seeing the solid figure of Locke unwavering before him, his mind instantly went to the Palace sculpture gardens and re-visited the images there of perfect and posed humans, so controlled, so calm, coolly accepting of their moments in the sun, on a pedestal, admired by all who passed by.

Air passed through his nostrils in a puff of loud air.

Dreams and desires were for fools.

When Wulf was silent too long, Malik leaned forward until his knees slid up and onto the bed. He knelt there, looking down at Wulf, his cigarette dangling between thin, firm lips. By the dim exterior lighting that slid through the big windows Wulf could see his eyes, a darkly, dangerous gray.

The man was not handsome like Locke, nor as refined, but his features were not unpleasant, a wide gaze, short cropped brown hair, and prominent cheekbones. His form was lean. He held himself up, looking down his nose at Wulf, body in perfect balance.

"There's no point in fighting. He will sell you either way, you know. Unless, well, unless you become an overnight prodigy, a genius pleasure slave like no other. But we both know that's not gonna happen." Malik spoke softly, as if he were sorry.

"If you want to win the bet, why are you telling me to stop fighting? Why are you telling me how to help Locke win?" Wulf's body went cold. A week ago he would have died for his cause. Now, so much weakness. Was he really afraid of dying?

"Oh, I don't care about the bet. But my friend has lost every bet we've ever shared together. Maybe I want him to see this through. Maybe I want him to be happy for a little while."

It didn't sound right.

"But you have to know," Malik continued, "so you're not disappointed in the end, he doesn't care. This was never a deal with the intention for him to keep you. Ours was a gentlemen's bet on a boring day when we both needed some excitement. Surely, that you can understand."

Malik's head bobbed. Wulf felt something sharp brush across his forearm where it lay against the bed spread. Ash. The cigarette, nearly forgotten, was burning up.

Malik's arm came up. A hand moved toward Wulf. He wanted to flinch. Instead, he forced himself to stay still.

Fingertips brushed against Wulf's shoulder, then his chest. Not even Locke had taken such liberties with him yet.

"Exquisite," Malik said. "If he truly does lose you by the tenth day, I would love to try you out for myself."

The hand moved up to cup the right side of Wulf's jaw. Wulf felt his own muscle move there, alongside the bone and up into his cheek. He had to concentrate to keep himself from swallowing the bile that came up in his throat.

Malik's palm was cool, rough. Not like Locke's gentle, quick touches when he'd helped Wulf up from the floor the first time he'd fallen, or helping him to regain his balance in the training room, or the warmth of his grip, slow and steady, when he held him through his second bout with the collar that had been turned off, and another fall.

He did not like this man's coldness. But then, he didn't have to. He was a slave. Such preferences did not come into his reality anymore. They were dismissed, unconsidered, invalid.

"I don't have to remove the covers to know what you look like. I've seen the majesty of your body. Everyone talks of

138

you in the halls. As you pass by, no eye stays away from gazing upon you."

"But that is all they can do. I belong to Locke." Again, he wasn't sure of the rules, but if he was wrong about this one, he had nothing to lose.

"He won't know, though. That I am here. That I have told you some of his secrets. That I have spared you distress by telling you of our bet, and that neither one of us really cares. For you won't tell him, will you? That I admire and want you? That even now I could fuck you into this mattress and your screams would fall on deaf ears."

Wulf's chest tightened. Would this man actually rape him? "H—how do you know he isn't watching right now?"

"I checked. Locke is asleep in his comfortable bed. For the time being. It gives us time."

The hand moved down to Wulf's chest again.

A whisper this time. "What is your desire? You should have something of it before you fail Locke entirely, before you die."

But not with you, Wulf thought.

Inside, he began to shake. But he kept his hands on top of the covers pressed down hard, steadying himself.

Malik leaned in further until Wulf could feel the man's smoky breath upon his face. The cigarette had gone out, fallen and lost in the wrinkles of the covers.

As the stranger's head moved down, so did his hand, brushing the tension of Wulf's flat stomach. He balanced on his knees. His free hand rose. In it, Wulf saw his leash. He'd taken it off before bed and hung it on the wall overhead. Malik had it now. And Malik was fastening it to his collar.

Wulf's blood ran cold.

Lips pressed lightly on Wulf's forehead. A kiss, cold and thin, cruel and thoughtless, but right at the juncture just above the eyebrows, a vulnerable spot where people touched out of affection, not disinterest.

There was no affection in Malik. None.

Wulf's fingers curled into fists. But he was afraid. The collar sat its weight on him. Was it on or off? Could Malik control its switches? Was Wulf brave enough to find out now that Malik held the leash?

It was attached now, but loose. As close as he was, Malik could yank it in a heartbeat.

Wulf could not control his shoulders from hunching. His legs bent to give himself more balance. He shrank back.

Malik's face moved forward, so close, staring at him, breathing on him, smelling of smoke and some sort of dusky cologne.

Malik's hand came up and touched the top of Wulf's head. Suddenly, the fingers wove into his hair, clenching, gripping. Wulf drew back.

"You do not get to do that."

"I am doing nothing," Wulf whispered.

"You are pulling away, my dear, rejecting. Hasn't Locke taught you anything?"

The grip on Wulf's hair tightened until Wulf had to tilt his head back to get relief.

He wanted to scream. *I thought you were waiting for Locke to lose your bet.*

Malik's hand followed the motion, tugging harder. "Oh but you will stay still, won't you? If Locke has taught you nothing, that collar has. Am I right? And if you don't perform well, and willingly, especially in this way, Locke will truly have no reason to keep you. Either way, you will probably be sold, but on the slim chance that you do well, perhaps your life can be extended. Or I could buy you after his failure and train you myself."

Wulf's glare tightened. His cheeks puffed out as he tried to control his breathing.

Malik came closer, lowering his head. His breath pulsed lightly against Wulf's lips. His face came ever closer.

Denial crashed through Wulf's system. But the risk-- He could take it. He *would* take it! He clamped down hard on

140

his internal muscles, shut his eyes tight and brought both hands up between them, shoving Malik back as hard as he could.

Malik gave a grunt, but that was nothing compared to the roar of his own voice as all his muscles began to cramp. Then came the pain, incredible surges of white hot electric fire stimulating his entire nervous system.

Wulf smelled burning, but not cigarette smoke this time. A taste of ash filled his mouth. He could not stop the screams that squeezed from aching throat muscles. He could not stop his body from convulsing.

Something hard hit him. The floor, perhaps, for there had been a brief moment he thought he was falling. He no longer knew his body, where it began, where it ended, only endless clouds of pain comprised his being, a torrent of red and black and oozing thick dark green.

It had never gone this far before. Always, before this point, the pain vanished. When Locke had been there, his soft hands held him as he regained his senses. Locke's warm chest had pressed briefly against his shoulders and back. His low voice had brought a stylized comfort that, even after only five days, Wulf had grown accustomed to. *You are safe.*

Where was that voice now?

His body arched up, the pain becoming a white reality of no return. A howling sound filled the area around him. He could not see or think, but he could still hear, still feel — it was too much.

When the screaming of his body and his world grew deafening, only then did blackness descend.

*

Wulf woke in a daze. At first his eyelids would not open. They felt glued shut. He tried to lift his hand to wipe away the stickiness but a stabbing in his forearm and bicep forced his hand back down under its own weight.

He was weak as a baby.

He shifted his legs. His thighs tried to cramp. After a few moments, his body aches receded and he could move easier. He rubbed his eyes and opened them. Sunlight streamed into them, stinging. When he tried to sit up, his stomach recoiled. Nausea swept through him.

He turned his head to look at the time. Locke would be arriving soon. He had to get up. But he couldn't muster the energy.

He managed to turn onto his side, pulling the covers with him. To his horror, as he turned he saw his leash curve about his body and begin to tighten.

Nothing happened.

Blinking, he stared at it before grasping it and wadding it into a ball against his chest. As he shifted his body to a more comfortable position, he heard something clatter against the floor. His phone.

He shut his eyes, sighing against the pillow. He didn't care. He wouldn't be needing it anyway in a few more days.

The next time he woke, Locke stood by the side of the bed. All Wulf saw at first was his black-clad thighs and groin. He lifted his eyelids up to the man's chest before they closed of their own accord.

Voices.

"His leash must have gotten tangled about him in his sleep and activated the collar."

"I only have the collar set to go off if he exits the room. He is allowed to take the leash off in his room. For some reason he didn't."

"Well, it must have been set wrong."

"I also didn't have the collar on high. Only on the lowest setting."

"Well, last night he experienced the high setting for at least a minute in duration. I can't say how long for sure, but his symptoms speak to at least that long. But he checks out fine. He'll be tired for a day, though."

142

Wulf realized the doctor had come into his room. It was his voice, his strangely cool demeanor that Wulf recognized. His covers had been pulled back. Gloved hands had probed. He remembered waking to it, feeling it but not understanding for long moments.

Wulf shuddered.

"Are you in pain?"

Wulf realized he heard Locke's voice. The master was addressing him. He couldn't yet answer.

"Wulf? How did this happen."

"No," Wulf finally managed, voice hoarse. "I don't feel pain anymore. Just aches." He reached for the leash he'd bound up by his chest and couldn't find it. Panic started to roll through him.

Locke said softly, "I took the leash off. No need to worry."

Wulf breathed out, body relaxing. It was the tone of voice he responded to as much as the words.

"Do you remember what happened?"

Wulf's body drew in on itself. He was shivering but before he could actually acknowledge the coldness coming up inside, Locke pulled the blanket over him.

"There. There." Locke said it twice.

"How did this happen, Wulf? Do you remember?"

Wulf shook his head, eyes opening slowly to take in the view of his master hovering over him, bending until he could finally see his face, those soft but dark eyes, the brown hair shining in the sunlight from the bared windows, his pink mouth down-turned in what looked like concern.

"I set the collar on low. After our scare yesterday, and we found out I'd forgotten to turn it on, I remember carefully setting it to low."

Wulf wanted to believe him. He did not want to think Locke was lying. But this man was also nobody to him. A stranger as of five days ago. A master of pleasure slaves. This man had bought him on a bet. This man was a great sinner.

But that voice… He could detect not one hint of dishonesty. In the tone he heard, unspoken, again and again: *You are safe.*

Locke reached out. He set his hand on the side of Wulf's head and gently stroked, fingers combing through his hair.

Wulf cringed. Jerked. "Don't."

Locke's hand lifted and cool air filled in where the hand had been. Wulf missed that warmth. But he couldn't take it. Malik's touch. Now this. If everything Locke had told him was a lie, he didn't want any touch. Or any reassurance. He was to die anyway.

But a part of him would not believe it. Locke had had no reason to lie. Malik had reason, though.

Wulf wanted to ask Locke about the bet but the words would not form.

"Rest," he heard his master say. "Rest."

Grateful for the fact that he did not have to move right now, Wulf did just that.

*

Every time he woke during the day, Locke was there with food or water or both. On through the dusk, Locke never left his side.

Well, that was something. Or maybe — everything.

Chapter Fifteen – Locke

What had happened to Wulf in the night had been a mistake. A mistake Locke had never made in his entire career, not even as a master-in-training. He had never left a collar on the high setting overnight. Not for any slave. Not for any reason.

He still wasn't sure this was *his* mistake, and his mind played over possibilities for an equipment malfunction.

And why hadn't Wulf taken off his leash before sleep? He'd been given permission to do so.

Wulf lay on his side, hands pulled up to his chest, knees bent.

Locke had folded the white sheet neatly over the edge of the blue spread and brought it up to the edge of Wulf's shoulder. Wulf's hair fell back from the side of his head and pooled in bronze curves against the white pillow. His breathing was smooth and even, now that the doctor had left.

The doctor had agitated him, but Locke insisted Wulf be checked out.

There had been no permanent damage from the collar going off for over a minute or more on the highest setting. But it had left Wulf listless, weak and tired.

Now Wulf slept.

Locke sat at the side of the bed in a chair, and turned on his phone.

He kept checking the video footage of the moment when Wulf had gone into convulsions. It was hard to see in the darkness, but he could make out the sheets and the bed and the single figure upon it.

The leash lay to the side of Wulf's body on top of the covers. All Locke could see was that sometime in the middle of the night Wulf had sat up, the leash had gone taut, and Wulf had begun to convulse.

The punishment lasted over a full minute, during which Wulf fell to the hard floor. Another camera angle took over from there, showing his body jerking helplessly, his limbs flailing.

Locke watched it again and again, looking for what might be missing. Looking for a reason that the leash would become taut. Maybe it had caught on something unseen. Maybe it wasn't that at all, and the collar simply short-circuited, then corrected itself.

He studied the other images in the room. Every once in a while, he glanced about the room as it appeared in the daylight, then went back to his phone and looked through the shadows from every camera angle.

Nothing.

No one had entered the room. Wulf simply sat up for a while, then went into convulsions and fell to the floor. When Locke sped the video up, he saw that later Wulf seemed to rise to his knees by himself and climb back into his bed.

Later, Locke planned to go to his private viewing alcove in his office and look at the bigger monitors. There, he could adjust the brightness, tweak the settings and maybe see more. For the moment, he refused to leave Wulf's side.

After about an hour, Locke got up and walked about the room, peering at the corners, the door, the carpet and tile. He glanced about the bathroom. Everything was clean, orderly. As it should be.

He walked around the bed.

Wulf moaned softly in his sleep and shifted.

Locke pressed his hand against Wulf's side over the covers, feeling the curve of his waist. "You are safe."

Wulf quieted. His breathing softened.

When Locke slid his hand back, his fingers encountered a small, soft object. He bent closer, picking it up.

In his palm lay a nearly burnt out cigarette stub, blackened on the end.

Had the doctor dropped this from a pocket or satchel as he was examining Wulf? He didn't know if Dr. Grunt—or rather, Dr. Torvalis—smoked or not. He'd never bothered to notice.

Maybe the cleaning crew had dropped it.

Well, this definitely was not Wulf's.

Locke pocketed the stub. Then he examined the bedcover. There was no burn mark. No ash. But he saw a darkened stain from the stub.

The idea that someone other than Wulf or himself or the cleaning crew had been in this room nudged his mind.

He had told Wulf he was safe. It was the truth. There were cameras everywhere. But—

His thoughts simmered darkly. Cameras could be tampered with. So could computers.

"Wulf," he whispered softly to the air. "What happened to you?"

Throughout the day, Wulf slept, rising only to pee, and once in the late afternoon, to take a quick shower. But he was still so worn out that Locke ordered him back to bed.

"We'll eat our dinner here," Locke said. "Are you up for a movie?"

"It's all pornography, isn't it?"

Locke laughed low in his throat. "No."

Locke prepared everything for the evening, including the ordering of a meal from the Palace kitchen. Warm soup. Cheese toast. Bright silver dishes of ice cream for dessert.

He dispersed with the TV locks that forbade Wulf from surfing channels, and brought up a movie.

As they began to eat, he turned to Wulf. "Before I start the movie, I have one question. Please try to answer truthfully if you can."

Wulf had brightened a bit after another nap. His blue eyes were no longer blood shot. But his gaze settled on Locke, closed and untrusting.

"Do you know of anyone who might come in here other than us? Other than the cleaners? Anyone who smokes?"

There was a moment of hesitation. Wulf's gaze dropped and his face notably paled. Though Wulf shook his head "no", that was all the answer Locke needed to know that told him someone had invaded Wulf's room and Wulf was lying to him about it. He didn't want to push Wulf. Yet. But he would get to the bottom of this.

For now, Locke pushed the start button on the movie.

He said, "This is *The Fast and the Furious*. Have you ever seen it?"

Wulf kept his eyes on his food and shook his head again. His broad chest rose and fell with quick, nervous breaths.

Well, the next couple of hours would be a good distraction for him.

"I think you'll like it," Locke said, and hit *play*.

*

"The time-date is rigged." The tech looked more like a movie idol than a computer expert, with his white-blond hair brushed up at the forehead, curving thickly against his temples toward the back of his neck. He was short, small, but perfectly proportioned.

The Palace kept civilians in its employ when necessary, people who were neither masters or slaves. People like Doctor Torvalis. And this man, Deke.

"Is there any way to know when or who did this?"

Deke shook his pretty head.

Locke sighed.

"I can tell the tampering was done from here and not somewhere else on the Palace computer systems. And that's probably why. None of the cameras seemed to be working in the hallway or in the slave's room at this time, no way to know who came in here and messed with your stuff. All the evidence would point to you doing the tampering since you're the only one with access."

"And yet it wasn't me."

"Do you have any enemies?"

Locke frowned. "No. And the Palace has almost zero crime. Minor incidents only. Everyone is vetted. And cameras are everywhere."

"Except in the private residences of Eminent Masters," Deke replied.

"Unfortunately, yes."

"Big Brother can't keep an eye on everyone, right? I mean, that would just be wrong."

Locke rolled his eyes. "The security system here is one of the most sophisticated in the world."

"I know. I help maintain it. But I'm afraid in this case, you're stuck."

"Thank you for your help." Locke walked Deke to his door.

For a long time he simply stood in the middle of his room staring at his computer alcove where the screens were lit, showing Wulf's room from all different angles. Wulf sat up in his bed watching the fourth installment of *The Fast and the Furious*. Locke had skipped the third as not worthy of watching and left Wulf to finish out the movie so he could meet the tech.

But he had no more answers than he did four hours ago.

Someone had to go to a lot of trouble to do this. Now Locke wondered, was the target Wulf? Or himself?

Chapter Sixteen – Wulf

The next day turned cold, and Master Locke took Wulf to the indoor galleries where the live human sculptures were displayed when the weather worsened.

Locke was placating him, no doubt, for the day Wulf had spent sick in bed. It was a neat trick. A ploy to make Wulf feel safe so he would cooperate and Locke would win his bet.

It was strange and unnerving that Locke was so solicitous after Wulf's punishment. But if he really wanted to show that he cared, he'd take the damn collar off Wulf. But that was never going to happen. Wulf was a slave until Locke was done with him, and then he would be sold with a file that marked him as dangerous and slated for a death penalty.

Why had Locke lied to him and told him otherwise? He didn't seem the type to stoop so low, to play such games, but then again, he was a master, an Eminent Master.

He had to be the best at what he did to claim that title. And that meant he was a manipulator of the highest regard. Someone who lorded his power over lesser beings, and was not only good at it, obviously enjoyed it.

As much as Wulf wanted to look at the sculptures, he forced his face forward and down-turned.

Locke said, as if he did not notice Wulf's indifference, "The groundskeepers work hard on the set up in here to make sure it reflects properly, everyone featured in their best light. They've done a good job, wouldn't you say?"

Wulf had ignored Locke's small talk at breakfast. After the movies last night, which he'd actually enjoyed, he was more determined than ever to reject Locke's overtures of friendship and pretend caring.

"Yes."

"You're not even looking," Locke said.

"Why are we here?"

"Because it's lovely and you like it."

"I want to go to the training room."

Locke let go of Wulf's leash. He circled around him.

Wulf kept his head down and did not look at him.

"Why?" Locke asked.

"I want to get all of this over with. Just—I don't want to wait any more!"

"I don't think you're ready."

Now Wulf lifted his head. He had to see the look on Locke's face. Was he joking? When was a slave ever ready to be raped?

"I am ready."

"I made a mistake in taking you there your first day out. I have re-considered your file and everything in it. I have not handled one such as you before, and so this is new for me, too."

To Wulf's mind, this was nonsense. It didn't matter anymore how Locke handled Wulf, as long as he got results quickly and forced him to perform for Malik in order to win his bet.

Wulf's body shook with a sudden tremor at the thought.

Instead of getting angry, Locke said, in his infuriatingly calm manner, "Do you need to sit down?"

"I'm fine."

Locke led Wulf through the giant room, the size of two large ballrooms, with high curved ceilings painted with bronze stars and moons, and pale walls trimmed in gold.

Only now and then did Wulf glance up. It didn't matter what he did, though, he would be sold.

But maybe, maybe if he performed well for Locke in the way of pleasure slaves, Locke would re-think his plan to sell him.

As the day went on, during swims, meals and Locke's desire to again tour classrooms—real classrooms—that taught everything from reading to history to advanced physics for slaves who showed any interest, all Wulf could think about was what Malik had told him.

He'd have to perform sexually, and in front of Malik, willingly. All for Locke to win the bet. If Locke won, maybe he wouldn't sell him.

Wulf shivered again. He should have welcomed death. He'd be a martyr to his people. And it was an easy escape from this surrounding insanity.

But now that he was well-fed, warm, with a comfortable bed, he'd turned weak. Yes, he did enjoy the sculptures. And swimming. And the movies last night. Locke's presence at his side all yesterday gave him a weird sense of security he'd never known.

Locke — who was going to sell him because he was a failure.

At dinner, Locke said, "You've been quiet all day. The night before last took its toll, I know. I have taken measures to make sure that never happens again."

They were in Wulf's rooms, as usual, sitting in their lounge chairs, eating and staring out at the city lights.

"Humph," Wulf said. He ate slowly, methodically, concentrating on every bite. But he could not distract his mind. He needed to train. He wanted to live.

Then the other proverbial ball dropped.

Locke said, quite matter-of-factly, "I know you have been dishonest with me."

The food Wulf was in the process of swallowing wanted to come back up. But he held it in, put down his fork and turned to Locke. He took several deep breaths.

"What is it?" Locke asked.

Wulf shut his eyes, opened them again. "I want you to bring me a consent form."

The fighter was gone. He was a disgrace. His own people would have instantly vilified him. Perhaps even imprisoned him. But everything was a trick. Everything. And he didn't want to die.

He watched Locke for a reaction. Only the eyes gave away any emotion with a dark flickering in their depths. As much as Wulf tried, he could not read Locke. He felt comfortable around him, but the new voices in his head told him it was all a ploy to win a bet.

Locke took a deep breath. "Why the sudden change of heart?"

"I've told you."

"Tell me again."

"I want it done. Over. That part, at least. So I don't have to think about it anymore. I want to know what's coming. I want it done." *And then maybe, just maybe, I'll live.*

"It's bothering you even more now, the training room."

How he always managed to turn Wulf's statements into weakness, Wulf didn't know. He wanted to deny it. Deny everything.

The lights of the city blinked like a strange, alluring seduction. White for purity. Green/gold for wealth. As if they were saying, *Look how beautiful we are, but you can never have us.*

That was Wulf's life now. Something lay before him that looked like a life. It breathed and moved and hungered and feared. It was never happy, but its instinct was still to survive.

And then there was Malik. Who could not be allowed to win. No more denial.

"Yes," said Wulf.

"Then perhaps you're not ready."

"But I must be. I can't bear waiting any longer." He must survive.

Locke sighed. An actual, long-drawn sigh. "Would you like to know what I've learned in the past few days with you?"

Wulf started to shake his head. He stared into his soup before he softly uttered, "What."

"You are not to be trained like the other slaves, for you are not like them. I was going to treat you like all the others. I was going to put you through all the motions, ignoring your file and all it said about you. But you aren't like them."

"Yes, I know. I'm being told constantly. I'm a danger. I should be put down."

"It means that I myself am experimenting with you."

Yes, Wulf knew this. The bet. The stupid, pervert friend. The outcome of being sold.

"I do not want to be an experiment," Wulf said. "I want consent forms. Then I want to be treated as any other slave here."

"You're not the master. You don't get to decide that."

Wulf faced him. "But do I get any say?"

"Of course you do. That is exactly why I said what I just said. You are not to be trained like other slaves."

"That is your decision?"

"Yes."

Wulf was silent. He didn't know what to think. Locke behaved often as if he actually liked him. He definitely wanted him. And there was that bet. So why not the training room?

"But," Locke continued, "on the matter of the consent form, if you are of sound body and mind, you may have one. Otherwise, it's not binding and we are back right where we started."

Well, Wulf didn't have a gun to his head. His body was healthy today. He was under duress, yes, and placed in a nightmare situation, but his days had, so far, been easy. And aside from Malik's intrusion, his nights had been undisturbed, peaceful.

The fact that impending death loomed over his head was the real reason he'd asked. Why could Locke not see that?

Perhaps he didn't care.

"I want to sign."

"I am reluctant. I think it's too early."

"It's not too early. I need to sign the form."

"This is against my better judgment. But if you think you need this, then tomorrow we'll go over paperwork. Then we'll see."

It would delay them further. Frustrated, Wulf said, "Why can't we do it tonight?"

"Because as your master I am ordering you to wait. If you are ready for consent, then you will not question my orders as a master to a slave."

Wulf said, glumly, "But I am ready now."

"You question me?"

"No, but I *am* ready."

Locke merely chuckled. "I have another movie to show you. *Not* pornography."

Which confused Wulf more, because why did Locke want to spend all his time with him? But when *Die Hard* began to play, he was riveted. He could not look away.

*

They sat at a long table in what looked like a boardroom. Files of papers, as well as two tablets, sat before Locke. Wulf felt entirely out of place, naked and ready to sign all his freedoms away forever. If, that was, he lived.

Two nights in a row now he'd slept with no interruptions. No Malik. Though Wulf had said nothing, security had improved. Or Malik had grown bored with the whole thing.

A solicitor had already been in, and gone through the long document marking each page Wulf was to sign. He would mark his thumbprint as well into the computer file on the tablet.

Wulf remembered signing papers to join the military in his home country. The documents were long and complicated. He had been eager to sign.

He was eager now but not for the same reasons. This needed to be done. What little control he had left of his life he wanted to keep. If he could convince Locke not to sell him —

"You can read it through if you like," Locke said. "Take your time."

Wulf ignored him and began signing and initialing at the highlight areas of each page. His eyes weren't working right anyway. The words were all blurred. With every signature, he felt stripped more naked than he had ever been. Invisible prison bars came down one by one disappearing into his flesh.

When he was finished, he pressed his thumb to the digital files. The solicitor gave his thumbprint, too, as legal counsel.

Locke gathered up the hardcopies and paper-clipped them, putting them neatly away in a red folder.

Wulf sat back in the chair. For a moment he did not know where to put his hands. He rested his palms on his bare thighs and looked up.

"Now can we go to the training room?"

Chapter Seventeen – Locke

The silvery light of the training room made Wulf's hair into a mix of platinums with variegated veins of amber.

Back straight, and deeply tanned from just one day at the outdoor pool, Wulf strode alongside Locke. The muscles along his spine all the way down to the curve of his firm ass rippled as he walked. He looked every inch a perfectly trained slave. His form was naturally beautiful, unforced.

Locke's throat tightened just to look at him. To hope.

But he could still feel it in his blood. Something was wrong. Despite all that Wulf had been through before coming to Avilan, something had happened to Wulf the night of his collar malfunction. Wulf wasn't talking. And Locke seemed to be the last person he wanted to talk to about it.

He had to think. Think about what he must order his slave to do. He had many choices. None of them right. But he had to start. Wulf wanted this. Wulf had given consent.

The training room was busy today. While the Palace did not adhere much to outside world daily schedules, Saturdays, Locke noted, were always like this. Maybe the crowds of slaves and the busy classes and bodies everywhere lounging, fucking, and being groomed would put Wulf at ease. But he thought not. For most slaves, he hoped the environment might become a painting they could blend into. It was Locke's experience that one did not feel so naked when everyone around them was naked as well. But Wulf was very different.

As they entered through the big double doors, Wulf's step skipped as if he almost tripped. As if the shock of the room's activities had physically pushed him off balance.

Locke did as he would with any slave; he leaned toward Wulf and said into his ear, "One step at a time. One thing at a time."

But Wulf, never one to obey, was glancing around the room, taking it all in at once. It was indeed a spectacle, a feast for the senses. Or an assault for those not used to it, for it was a lot to take in all at once.

Nearly every alcove was occupied with two to four people at a time. The stage rocked with slaves prancing up and down the walkway, or sitting on the sides grooming, braiding hair, caressing pert breasts or erect penises.

Large screens overhead depicted close up videos of sexual acts between all genders.

Dark-clad masters peppered the room, overseeing the naked slaves and their acts. Some masters remained fully dressed — as Locke preferred for the simple reminder of the power play between master and slave — while others were shirtless. The masters who chose to be as naked as their trainees could be identified by the busy-belts they still wore about their waists.

In the first alcove, only a few feet away from them, a male master was instructing a male slave in the art of anal intercourse.

"But I'm a virgin; it will hurt," the slave insisted with beautifully down-turned eyes.

The master replied, "Not after I'm done thoroughly preparing you."

The slave lay on his back on the bed amidst the reds and lavenders of luxurious spreads and pillows, naked and aroused as his master standing over him gave him a massage with copious amounts of oil and continued to instruct him on how relaxed his muscles would become, and how addicting the milking of the prostate gland could be. By the time his erect cock penetrated him, the master promised the slave would experience utter bliss.

Wulf's face darkened at the overheard conversation but he gave no other indication of his discomfort.

The room buzzed. Voices echoed off the high ceilings and wide walls. As they moved forward, other snippets of conversations could be heard. A teary slave: "But I came too fast." And another, excited: "Can we try it again?"

Scents wafted by of various mixtures of fruits from the scented lubes the Palace provided, as well as powders, paints and hair gels used by slaves and masters alike to decorate their bodies more erotically. The adjoining bath area was also busy as slaves came and went from the more than a dozen shower stalls within. Hygiene was encouraged. On the weekends, the showers almost constantly ran.

It had been a week since the new batch of slaves Wulf had come in with had arrived. There had been no new batches since. So today the room was bright, the mood up. There was evidence of very little cowering or shyness as the newest and oldest mixed, all having had time to acclimate themselves to their new lives.

Wulf had not been among them. While the newest slaves were always required to attend training room sessions at least twice a day, Wulf had only been to this part of the Palace once. That meant even the greenest of the newbies here today had twelve to fourteen times more experience with this room than Wulf.

They needed it, too, in order to understand what would be required of them when they were finally sold.

However, Wulf did not need this if he didn't really want it. Not anymore. Not since Locke had reevaluated his reasons for buying the man and wanted to keep him. Technically, Wulf was not being groomed for any of the futures these slaves faced. All Wulf needed to do was please Locke, and his existence already did that.

Locke had tried to be clear on this with Wulf. During the signing of the consent forms, he'd told Wulf, "You don't have to do this. You are my slave. I bought you. You belong to me, not the Palace. I will force you into nothing."

But Wulf did not seem to hear him.

It seemed Wulf did not hear a lot of what Locke said to him. And Locke had to remind himself that Wulf's will

159

needed training more than anything else. He didn't want to break the man, but he did need him to behave if for no other reason than the comfort of Wulf himself. He needed to understand what was expected of him so he would not be surprised by so much, so his rage did not take over and make life miserable for himself and all around him.

Yes, Wulf did indeed need to learn how to behave. And to trust.

The training room was excellent for dealing with trust issues. It wasn't all about technique and fucking. The art of love-making was also part of the weave, intrinsic to many human souls. That included emotions — whether you wanted them to be part of it or not, but in Locke's experience they still must be dealt with.

Some slaves were in the training room as workers today. They rushed around cleaning alcoves, changing bed linens, mopping the bathrooms.

Small green lights above the alcove entrances indicated the alcove was empty and fully cleaned.

Locke spotted one, picked up Wulf's leash which had been dangling limp at his side, and led him to it.

Wulf's embarrassment turned to fear for a moment as all the pink drained from his face.

"Do you not want to go to an alcove?" Locke asked.

But Wulf was staring at the leash.

"Ah." He tilted his head, trying to get Wulf to look at him. "The leash is on the lowest setting. I promise. I've triple-checked. I even had the controller replaced. After what you went through, I would use another method of restraint, but the rules of the Palace are strict about collars. They must be worn by slaves at all times."

Wulf nodded, then said in a dead tone, "I do not object to the alcove."

The din from the training room receded with three walls enclosing them. There was no ceiling to the alcove, but the noisy surroundings diminished.

160

Locke would have preferred a private room. Perhaps even his own. A public training room was a society of sorts and not for everyone, though most slaves enjoyed it once they got past their inhibitions.

"I have to ask you again, Wulf," Locke said. "Why did you insist on coming here when I have not ordered you to?"

"Because I want to learn and learn fast."

"So suddenly?"

Wulf gave only a nod in response.

Both wary and slightly endeared, Locke said, "All right. What would you like to learn first?"

"I—I—figure you have a plan with all your slaves."

"I have not done hands-on training in a while. Perhaps I forgot to say that in our conversations. Also, every slave is different in their files from life experience to gender orientation to wide ranges of personality. I told you I had made a mistake in bringing you here your first day."

"It was not your mistake, it was mine." Wulf appeared to be struggling a bit with his words. "I was unable to express to you what I was and was not—ready for."

"All right. The video I wanted to show you was merely educational. But it was too fast. And I think you do not need it at this point. That is my assessment on this day. That may change."

Wulf nodded. His eyes were unsteady, but he kept his head up.

"So with someone such as you, who is untried, I often start with a massage."

Wulf took a breath but said nothing.

Locke continued. "Normally I would call upon my best slave masseuses in the Palace and observe the action on the slave."

Wulf shook his head. "You mean a massage for me? I thought you meant I should massage you."

"I meant a massage for you."

"But I should be learning to pleasure you. I should be giving you the massage."

"As your master, I say no."

"But--?"

"No," Locke cut him off.

Wulf's gaze flickered toward the bed. "I don't under—"

Locke interrupted him again. "You do not have to understand. On the bed." Locke held the leash out. "I will give you this to hold if you obey me."

Wulf reached out and took his own leash. Slowly, he backed onto the bed and sat. One by one, he lifted his long, gorgeous legs onto the mattress, his hands behind him, palms flat on the spread to hold himself up. His shy cock hid between his legs, still impressive even flaccid because of its length.

The body sprawled out before Locke was too beautiful for words. It was his. But it was not his.

"On your stomach," Locke said.

A hesitation.

"This will not work if you do not want to do this."

"It will," Wulf insisted. "But I want to learn to please." The pleading look in the pale blue eyes appeared honest. Open. It was the first time Locke had seen that look on Wulf.

"You learn first by obeying your master's orders."

"Yes, but—"

"On your stomach."

Wulf arranged himself as ordered, his arms trembling along his sides. One leg bent slightly, as if to ease a silent stress in his lower back.

Locke did not make him straighten the leg. The massage would either calm him or rouse him or both.

Locke rolled up his sleeves, talking as he did so. This would be the first time he would be touching Wulf beyond steadying him, or helping him stand after falling.

"What happened with your collar has stiffened your muscles. This will be a treatment in addition to a part of your training to loosen up, and it will allow faster healing."

"And the training part?" Wulf asked.

"To test to see if you can allow my touch."

"I will allow it," Wulf said, turning his cheek into the pillow.

"You say that with your mind. Will your body make the same statement?"

"Body and mind are connected."

"Sometimes," Locke replied, reaching for the oil.

"I want you to train me."

The desperation Locke heard in that voice bordered on fear. The malfunction of the collar had traumatized Wulf, certainly, but there was more.

Locke squirted oil on the broad back, prepared to learn more.

Wulf's skin twitched as the oil hit him. It was cooler than body temperature and probably felt cold as it sprayed him.

Locke placed his hands flat on Wulf's upper back, pushing against the firm muscle over the shoulder blades and onto the shoulders. Then he moved them back down, spreading the oil, watching as it glistened up between his fingers.

He looked down toward Wulf's buttocks, their perfect curves, the firm, bronze skin. His breath caught in brimming desire.

He let his hands sink into the silken skin, his mind flooded with images of Wulf sitting up in his bed, his body convulsing, falling, his mouth open in agony. He should have been there. He should have better protected his slave.

His hands trailed down Wulf's spine. His slave sighed.

"Wulf."

"Hmm."

He pressed into the spine, gentle but firm, running his fingertips over each disk.

"I want to know about that night."

The body beneath him tensed. "What night?"

"The night your collar malfunctioned."

"I don't remember much. Just pain. And being very tired."

"There is more."

Wulf did not answer.

"Did anyone come into your room?"

"I don't remember."

"Relax and let your thoughts go. Try for me, all right?"

The body beneath him went taut, then relaxed. The word "Yes" came out as a breath more than a tone.

Locke continued the massage in silence. Only the outside din of the training room could be heard, a slightly muffled roar of human voices talking all at once, some laughter, some groans and moans, a few shouts of ecstasy.

For the first time in his life, Locke felt greedy. He did not want to be here among others. He did not want to share Wulf in such a public venue. He wanted all their times from now on, now that Wulf had signed the consent papers, to be private.

But how could he say that with Wulf now begging to be trained? He did not want to wreck this fragile new change of Wulf suddenly wanting to fit in and do well. To change.

It all seemed too good to be true.

"Are you remembering anything?" Locke asked.

The muscles under his hands tensed again.

"No," came the strained voice.

Locke sighed.

Chapter Eighteen – Wulf

"Are you remembering anything?" Locke asked.

Wulf had never had a massage before. The hands on his body, so warm, so amazing—like nothing he'd ever felt—had put his mind at ease for a few minutes. That one question jerked white light through his brain. A shock.

For a second, he did not understand the words even though he knew he should have been thinking about them. Per his master's orders.

"No."

It was the wrong answer. He knew that. He was lying. He remembered Malik threatening him that he would be sold no matter what. And that matters would only be worse if he told Locke about what Malik had said.

The warmth against his back increased. The tempo of Locke's stroking hands went faster. Locke leaned into his work, obviously knowing what he was doing.

It felt so good!

He did not want to think about Malik. Only Locke. Only Locke's hands. They did not feel like sin. Locke had only been kind to him. When he thought of Locke, and when he was with him, he felt safe. But that was an illusion.

The hands, the pressure moving over him, the fingertips finding those places where he didn't even realize he'd been hurting or tense, made his body buzz with an internal longing he'd felt only in his deepest, most secret fantasies.

Something in his body was connecting to those hands. And his mind wanted to allow it. Wanted more.

He breathed deep. The pillow smelled of soap. The oil on his back was woodsy, like sandalwood or cedar. A comforting fragrance reminding him of more innocent times, when he was a child and his father was distant and he could play freely. Before he knew of war and humiliation, fighting and the sins of the body.

Locke's voice came as if from far away. "Did a sound wake you first? For you were sitting up before the collar malfunctioned."

"No."

Locke's hands moved further down, almost touching his buttocks. A part of Wulf wanted Locke to touch him there, stroke gently at first, then harder. His body went liquid and warm at the thought. A surge of heat went through his abdomen, leaving behind churning warmth.

But Locke avoided that part of him, moving onto the backs of his thighs, which was nice, too, and made him relax.

"Did you smell anything on the air? Smoke, maybe?"

Now Wulf tensed. For Malik had been smoking. How could Locke know?

"No," he lied.

Abruptly, Locke seemed to change the subject. "You may be please to know, I'm an expert at giving massages. I learned long ago, when I was still very young."

Wulf shut his eyes tight and breathed in the comforting pillow scent.

"The body telegraphs signals all the time, did you know?"

Wulf gave a grunt. But he was actually loving this. The hands, the tone of Locke's deep voice. The way his world seemed to be floating as he forgot, for this moment in time, his inhibitions, and his sense of injustice and rage at life, the universe and everything.

"Electrical impulses. Fluctuations in temperature and muscle. If you map it with your hands and you are expert at reading the signals, you can tell many things. Like when someone is lying, for example."

The floating world vanished. Wulf felt this toes flex. His calves wanted to cramp.

"Ah," Locke said. "I hit a nerve here just above the knee, I think."

Was Locke being sarcastic? Playing games?

Wulf forced himself to keep his breathing even and shallow. He had been lying. To his master. This was not how he should make his new start if he wanted to live. But he could not make himself speak the truth.

Malik could find out and then say anything. It would be Wulf's word against Malik's. He was nobody. Malik was a master. Wulf would lose. Wulf would be sold as a disobedient slave, a liar, if he could not please Locke and show him he was worth keeping. Worth owning.

"Training begins with trust." Locke's words fell across Wulf's back like light and warmth. The hands pressed more tension away.

"If you don't trust your master," Locke continued, "you will falter. Always. But not all masters are trustworthy. That is a fact. We are human. But here at the Palace, we work hard to make the community strong. The lessons in training are less about criticism and more about highlighting assets, strengths, and praising what you do well."

Wulf believed Locke believed what he was saying. But Wulf was not a Palace slave. The circumstances for him were different. To be labeled a One-Night Thrall was disastrous.

When he'd been captured and fought, and during his days in the military prison, he didn't care what happened. He had told himself death was his only option. He could be a martyr.

He convinced himself his fate would put an end to this hell. But only six days here at the Palace and he saw death as one option only. An option he no longer accepted. With all his soul, he did not want to face that. He wanted Locke to see he was worthy. He wanted to be the best.

In a way, it wasn't fair that Locke refused to train him like the other slaves.

Wulf moved as Locke's fingers woke him again from his reverie, skimming his calves, almost tickling. He wanted to turn over, sit up, but he also wanted those hands on him, and more words in the way Locke spoke them, like a prayer.

"Easy. Lie still."

Wulf only now realized he'd lifted his arms to push himself up. He fell forward again, crossing his arms underneath his face in a more comfortable position.

"Lie still," Locke repeated.

Heat ran through Wulf at the words *Lie still*. He wasn't sure why. But the combination of those words, the command of them, and their meaning eased him into a quiet peace. They filled him with something else, too, an erotic promise he found he wanted despite the old voices in his head that forbade such feelings.

Despite the idea that he might be disobeying some other, deeper, unseen voice that told him he was bad. If a master commanded him to lie still, then he needed to take no responsibility for what happened.

It was freeing.

"Will you tell me," Locke asked, "what you are thinking right now this very moment?"

Wulf's eyes flashed open. He couldn't. Could he?

"There are no wrong answers." Locke's hands had reached Wulf's feet and were massaging the ankles, the heels, the instep, first one foot, then the other. Wulf wanted to arch at the pleasure of it. He held still.

The silence stretched between them.

"No thoughts?" Locke pressed gently at the ball of Wulf's left foot. "Anything that comes to mind is welcome."

Wulf wanted to be right, to be good.

"That I am bad." But no, he should not have said that. That was too dark, too negative. "That when you told me to lie still my body wanted to uh, maybe... dissolve?"

"Thank you for your honesty. Was that the first time?"

"First time?"

"That you haven't told me what you think you should be telling me, or what you think I want to hear."

"I don't know—" Wulf didn't know. He had not been in tune with his heart, only his intellect. Since childhood, he'd thought his way through every predicament. Feelings were never to be taken into account. Outbursts in children were severely punished.

"What do you know now?"

"That I want to be good for you as a slave. I want you to see that."

"Why? Why have you changed so quickly? Can you tell me that?"

"I want to fit in here." Now he was lying again. He didn't want to fit in. He wanted to live.

Locke chuckled. "I do not think that is true. Try again."

"I—I—" Frustration clenched in Wulf's throat and chest. He moved his head up, his hands pushing against the pillows.

Locke's hands moved to his hips. He did not touch Wulf's buttocks, only the sides of his upper thighs, and the dent of his hips where they met his torso. Thumbs caressed close against his lower back. Locke was efficiently cupping his waist.

"What is it you're trying to tell me?" Locke's hands came up quickly to Wulf's neck, pushing gently.

"Down, down," Locke said.

Wulf pressed his forehead into his arms again. "I—I— don't want to die. If I am of value, I could maybe stay alive." He gulped.

Locke did not seem at all surprised or flustered. Only calm as he worked kinks from the back of Wulf's neck.

Locke said, "I have told you you are safe. Yet you do not believe me."

Wulf groaned. The fingers felt so good.

"Truth, please," Locke said.

Wulf shut his eyes tight. Held his breath.

169

"Nothing?"

Through gritted teeth. "I don't know."

"You don't know if you can believe me."

Louder. "I don't know!"

"Then the trust between us is not established."

Failure.

Wulf started to deny it. "That's not — that's unfair."

"How does fairness come into play? It's what is. You do not trust me."

Locke's fingers furrowed in the hairline at the base of Wulf's neck. His blond hair, parted, hung on either side of his jaw. The master's fingers pressed up, weaving themselves into his locks.

Sparks stirred in Wulf's stomach, a fluttering of individual heated points within. The sensation moved up and down his body, but most of it centered at his groin as his cock pressed against the spread with an overwhelming ache. His balls shifted and he lifted his hips to ease the pressure.

The sandalwood scent of the oils and the fresh-air fragrance of the pillows mixed with the musk of arousal. Wulf's mind whirled.

He was supposed to be arousing his master, wasn't he? He wanted to learn the art of pleasure, not this — this feeling. It was too intimate, too revealing. His clothing had been stripped away, but this was more stripping, as if his skin was sloughing off. The vulnerability of helplessness before all options of loss and more loss hurt but the arousal deepened. It was too much.

Locke said, "Hmm," and nothing more.

Wulf lifted his hips a second time. Adjusting, but his cock only grew warmer.

"It's not fair," Wulf began. "Because — " He gulped. "Because you won't train me like the others so I am doomed to fail anyway. If I fail, you will be displeased. Why keep me then?"

170

A lot of his words muted themselves as he spoke into the pillow.

"I see. Good questions. Did you think of them on your own?"

"But your bet—" And now he'd said it. What he wasn't ready to reveal. But the hands had relaxed him so much.

They continued to stroke him on his neck and shoulders.

As if nothing had been revealed that Locke didn't already know, Locke said, "I see. You know that the bet is between me and Malik. No one else. Not even you. You are not responsible for my actions, or my choices. I am the master here. You are responsible only for obeying me. You still have not learned the lesson."

Had Malik talked to Locke? Did Locke already know Malik had assaulted him in the night? This made things far worse.

Wulf could not move. The hands on him were too relaxing. Fingertips scraped lightly against Wulf's scalp. His body felt hot all over, slick from more than oil. He sweated, seethed, wanting to move, to feel and not feel. Which?

His hair ruffled at Locke's ministrations. His nostrils filled with the perfumes of pleasure. He tasted something sweet in the back of his throat. He was a prude, he knew it, but this wasn't new. He'd come before with his own hand. Just not often, and too often quite unwillingly. He used his petal often and it helped.

Locke said he wasn't responsible, but he couldn't think. A petal would help him think. Before he knew it, he was saying it aloud. "If I had a petal, it would help."

"What is a petal?" Locke asked calmly.

It was the most erotic feeling, those fingers in his hair, moving in slow circles, pressing in all the right places.

Wulf realized now that he would have to explain. He couldn't. But of course he could.

Locke was a master of pleasure slaves. He'd seen it all. He'd heard it all. But he did not know what a petal was.

"It's-- it fastens onto a man." Wulf shifted against the spread and the sparks grew into conflagrations. His cock tingled. "And a chain pulls it back and fastens to a belt."

"It? What?"

"It forces an—an erection down. I need one." On that last word, his voice quivered and came out too high.

"Oh, you are describing a cock cage." Locke said this so matter-of-factly that Wulf shut his eyes tight enough to see red explosions on the insides of his eyelids.

"You have worn a cock cage before?" Locke asked.

"Yes," Wulf replied in a small voice.

"Often?"

"Off and on since I was fourteen."

"What?" Locke's hands came away from Wulf's head. He heard Locke move closer to the head of the bed, heard the rustling of clothing as he bent down. A hand touched him at the center of his damp back, slippery but at ease.

Wulf whispered into his arms. "All boys wear them."

"No," Locke said softly. "No, they don't."

Locke's hand slid down Wulf's back, a gentle stroking.

Then Locke asked, "That night when your collar malfunctioned. Is that when you learned of the bet?"

Wulf couldn't answer. Didn't care anymore.

Oh, it was like flying. That hand on him, the gentleness and the feeling of gloss and smoothness. Wulf's muscles rippled.

The pressure in his cock intensified. Burning sensations all over his body trapped him in a sort of bliss and terror at the same time, for he was on the verge of coming and it couldn't happen like this. It was just a massage. He had not even turned over to show his vulnerable underbelly yet.

"I need a petal. I need it now," Wulf said.

"A petal. Hmm," Locke's hand would not stop. "I don't think so. It would mar the beauty of you completely, the utter purity of your response. Don't you think?"

"No. It's not pure. It's not pure, it's—"

"Shhh."

The bed shifted and Wulf realized Locke had settled himself on the edge. The side of his pant leg brushed Wulf's thigh.

"But I— I need you to win the bet."

"It is not for you to worry about. Have I not told you? You are safe here. With me."

Wulf lifted his head and turned it, trying to see Locke at his side. He wanted to look into his eyes. To know. Was he telling the truth?

Locke's knee was close to Wulf's nose. He inhaled the man's scent, the cleanness of him, the clothing fresh and laundered, a singular scent he could not name that was Locke's alone, a fresh almost-sweetness. He hungered for it. But the more he hungered, the greater his arousal flared.

His gaze was blurred. He blinked and blinked, trying to clear it. But Locke's hand up and down his back made his eyes roll up.

And then Locke's words, "Don't you realize how beautiful you really are?"

He was a fighter. A warrior. A nobody. He could be sacrificed for his country's cause at a whim. He wasn't beautiful. He was just a machine.

But Locke made his body believe. For a second, *he believed.*

"On your side," Locke commanded thickly.

Wulf suffered to obey. Tried to roll. His trapped cock sprung up before he could draw his knees up.

And to his horror, as it dipped back to smack his stomach, that single movement alone stimulated the heat to a white-hot burn. His arm went down but not fast enough to grab himself. Locke caught his wrist, held it, and looked into his eyes.

Wulf groaned and everything came apart, turned into stars and crashing planets, white sheets of hot rain and fire. Everything fell to pieces around him. Including his soul.

His cock spasmed. The flaming fluid of his ejaculation spurted against his thigh and stomach, and no doubt onto the spread as well.

He'd messed up bad. So bad.

He gasped in shock at himself, the air rasping like sand in his throat. Hot breaths of air gushed from his mouth. "Oh, I—I didn't mean to, I—" He couldn't find words.

He ripped his wrist from Locke's grip, putting his hand to his face as if to hide like a stupid child. His cheeks were wet but he didn't know when that had happened. It was all like a horrible dream.

"Please don't sell me!" said a voice that sounded very much like his own. "Don't sell me! I didn't mean to. I didn't mean to."

Ok, so he could still talk. He had to get hold of himself. He had to fix this. It was fixable. Locke had certainly seen it all, including failed slaves.

"I'll do better, I promise! Just don't make me be a—a thrall for one night for strangers, I—I—"

"Shh. I won't sell you. Do you hear me now? I won't sell you."

Locke's words sounded hollow to Wulf's ears. He was lying. Malik said so. This was all for a bet. All for a bet and Locke was going to lose. And Wulf was going to lose, too. Lose everything.

Chapter Nineteen – Locke

"I beg you, please."

Wulf seemed to be trying to right himself onto his knees, so out of place, so wrong, and Locke would not have it. But no matter how hard he tried, he could not get his slave to relax.

"Why would you think I am going to sell you? Have I not told you over and over you are mine now?"

"For ten days I'm yours. That's all. I know —" Wulf's breaths came slower now as he got control of himself.

So beautiful, he was, his cock still hard, the pink tip wide and engorged, dripping. How spectacular he'd been, coming from just a touch to his back.

Locke said, "That's how long the bet was for, yes. But not how long I own you. I already told you, the bet is not your responsibility. It's mine and I will deal with it. The winning and the losing have nothing to do with you. I have bought you in a final sale. You are mine. How many times do I have to explain this?"

"But — but I am all wrong, not working right in my head or my body — broken. Obviously, you can't keep me. Not here in the Palace. Not anywhere. But I am trying — trying to do better. I can do better!"

To hear Wulf's voice hitch and pant, to watch him hold back the tears of horror and mortification he must be feeling made Locke frustrated and angry and sympathetic all at once. He wanted to take the man and shake him, make him see how beautiful he was, how perfect with his fighting nature and proud denials. To see how brutally and honestly Locke had fallen for him like no other slave he'd ever met.

For he had fallen. And fallen hard. This man's anger and passion and denial made him glow.

"Sweetheart, you do not have to try to do better for me. You are the one who wanted to be brought to the training room."

"Yes! Because I want to learn to do this right. I want you to keep me."

"I am already keeping you."

But Wulf's breathing came hard again, and he seemed not to hear him.

Locke put both hands on Wulf's slippery shoulders, gripping tight. "Listen to me! I am keeping you."

Wulf looked up at him. "Ten days only," he said. "Ten days."

"Someone other than me has put this notion into your head. Who said that to you?"

But there was only one person it could be. He suspected. But now he knew for sure. Malik.

"Come," Locke said, moving forward and off the bed, standing. He grabbed Wulf's leash.

Wulf recoiled.

"Stand. I'm taking you back to your room."

Wulf shook his head. "Please. Can we try again?"

"A massage? No."

"Not for me. For you. Please. Let me." Slowly, Wulf got to his feet, his body gleaming with oils. His cock had lost its lovely fullness — how alluring and virile this man was! — but still so beautiful nestled and half-hard in its golden glistening curls.

"I am to walk through the halls like this?" Wulf asked, mouth open in horror.

Locke took pity, handing him a towel. He said, "If a master asks you to walk through the halls like that, you must do so. Is that the training you are asking for?"

Wulf's face pinked.

Locke's gaze softened. "Trust," he said. "Your first lesson. Do you understand now?"

Wulf looked up, lashes catching the edges of bluish light that rained down from the high ceiling overhead. "I failed."

"Oh, no, my proud warrior, *my slave*. You did better than anyone who has gone before you as my trainee. You have moved me."

The towel dangled from Wulf's grip. His mouth opened, the pink lips full and perfect, framing such a handsome mouth. As if a magic wand had been waved, all the muscles of his face and torso relaxed. If possible, he became even more stunning and alluring than ever to Locke.

Locke stepped forward until his mouth was only inches from Wulf's. Their eyes met. Locke whispered with all the reverence he could muster.

"This is the final time I will say this. I will *never* sell you."

*

How could he tell Wulf everything that was in his heart? For a master, it was unthinkable. He'd been taught early on to distance connections with slaves even as he taught them to trust him.

By his own will, he could have lovers, of course. But he'd had only trysts. Nothing with staying power. His heart was a ghost because of it.

But Wulf was his slave. His own by choice. He could tell him everything. He wanted to. The ghost of his heart was already revived. He could tell him that. But perhaps not in those particular words.

Locke had tasted the elixir of eager slaves, wrestled with the sad ones, clinked wine glasses with the dejected ones, spent all night fucking sessions with the insatiable ones. He'd drowned in pillows of pleasure until he could not breathe.

When he became an Eminent Master all that stopped. It wasn't required that he stop his hands-on training, it was a choice. He still took on trainees, but he had other trainers handle them physically. He directed, he taught, he watched. He had asked himself why he stopped having physical sex with his trainees about a million times. All he could think was that it had become such a routine for him, and only deepened some inner longing he could never define.

Surrounded by people and sex, he had not thought of himself as lonely.

Not until Wulf fell into his arms. Standing before him in the training room alcove, pink in the cheeks, the blush spreading in a lovely oblong pattern on his chest, Wulf looked helpless and ready to fight and vulnerable and wanting all at once. And oh, so desirable.

Locke had to get his nervous slave in hand.

He loved watching the blues of Wulf's eyes darken with emotion. Emotion Wulf pretended not to have. Everything in Locke stirred for this man.

A half-step back and Locke picked up Wulf's leash, handing it to him.

The slave stood motionless before him, towel hanging in front of his groin.

"Come," Locke said in his most commanding tone. But he kept his voice soft.

Deciding Wulf would follow, for he always did now even when Locke had told him his collar was off, he turned and walked out of the alcove and into the din and crowd of masters and slaves.

So many naked bodies, so much beauty. Locke never tired of the sight. But as he'd grown older, he was quickened by other things: an autumn leaf falling against a clear blue sky, the sculpture gardens on Halloween, a long novel about reluctant princes and asshole kings, his own deep dreams, which he could almost touch but left him reaching blindly for his tossed off blankets.

Could he ever confess *that* to his slave?

He moved quickly past the stage with the throngs of slaves waiting in line for something—a turn to prance and preen on high for there was some kind of show being put on center-stage right now.

Locke kept his gaze fixed on the ornate double doors. He could feel Wulf behind him, probably still carrying his beloved cleansing towel. Wulf who was heart-stopping in his innocence and beauty, and who had cried for a cock-cage.

Wulf was his now, if only he could make him believe. The thought sent shocks of pleasure through his veins. His balls twitched. His cock was already hard and had been for some time.

The double doors opened. Through the hallways, ignoring his peers and their slaves, Locke walked, Wulf trailing behind him.

He wished he could see the image of his fantastic and magnificent naked slave following him. The one who, at first, had been so angry. So fierce.

And oh, Wulf was still fierce.

Wulf was only just getting started in his training.

Locke wanted to make him show that strength. All the time. Locke loved that about him almost as much as his sweet outrage, and his firm golden ass and big cock.

Locke led Wulf back to his slave suite. It was still early, but Wulf deserved a break.

Wulf looked at him with questions as they walked into Wulf's room, but remained quiet.

"You may shower if you like," Locke told him. "You may watch a movie. I have some things to attend to, and then I will return."

Relief made Wulf's eyes soften. He nodded, his mouth set into a firm line.

"Relax," Locke added. "That's an order. I'm not leaving you. But I must attend to a matter."

Wulf nodded and turned toward the bathroom.

Locke left and locked the room with a new personal code. Next, Locke grabbed his tablet from his belt and turned it on as he walked. A few quick touches to the screen and he had completed his task.

He gave a verbal order to his tablet and it replied with the desired response. He moved toward the masters' general viewing rooms.

In less than a minute, he arrived. He was not surprised at what greeted him.

"I knew I'd find you here, Malik." Locke strode forward to view the screen Malik was so intent on.

Malik turned abruptly. To cover his surprise, he sent Locke a lazy smile. A cigarette glowed at the edges of Malik's thumb and forefinger. Malik always held his cigarettes that way, as if he wanted them to burn down until they touched the skin.

"What are you doing?" Locke asked, even though he already knew the answer.

It was not forbidden for other masters to view any slave from this area, but Locke had had Wulf's on a private setting. That meant Malik had hacked them. He had the skill. The Palace tech might not have thought to mention it if he'd found the cameras accessed from the main area. The question they'd investigated was that the cameras had been turned off, not that they'd been viewed from other areas.

Wulf's rooms showed in full color on two large screens from two different angles. The slave paced before the long front windows of the living area, turning occasionally to look out. The afternoon had grown overcast. The city far below Palace grounds looked dusty, unkempt. The glittering jewels of nighttime lights were gone during the day, making it all far too ordinary.

"Looking at your prize," Malik replied. "I am allowed, aren't I? He is certainly no secret you are keeping."

Wulf had taken off his leash. It hung on its special hook by the bed. He moved about the room, exuding restlessness.

180

Locke couldn't help but note the natural grace of the man, how he moved cat-like with perfect posture and form.

"This is a private setting you're using. Mine. These cameras in Wulf's room are not public slave cameras."

"I know that. But we're friends. I didn't think you'd mind so much if I looked for a minute. Pardon me."

"Checking up on him?"

Malik spread his hands as if surrendering to Locke's position as Eminent Master. As well he should, Locke thought.

Malik said, "Just wanted to see how things were going."

"Yes, our friendly wager. Did you spy upon the two of us in the training room as well?"

Malik smiled. "I'm no stalker."

"I disagree."

"What?" Malik's lips made an exaggerated pout.

Locke held out the tablet he carried. "I have taken the liberty of transferring the wager from our bet into your account."

Malik took the tablet from his hand and looked down. "Money? You paid me the money from our bet already? So sure you've already lost, eh?"

"Yes. I am. So you can stop spying."

"I wasn't spying—"

"Oh, yes," Locke interrupted. "One more thing. It is against Palace law to let yourself into a slave's quarters without permission from the primary master. But in this case, I'm not just Wulf's master, I'm his owner."

"I have no idea—"

"And tampering with camera footage. That's a premeditated act of trespassing. Trespassing on my property."

"I didn't—"

"I always suspected you had visited Wulf. When I found your cigarette stub was when I became more sure, but I didn't want to believe it of a man I thought was my friend. What did you say to him? Did you dare to touch him?"

Malik raised an eyebrow.

Shaking his head, Locke said, "I've known you forever, it seems. Malik, we were friends."

"We still are. It was just a friendly wager, that's all, and he's just a One-Night Thrall. You yourself said you've already lost our bet. You can't tame him. It's impossible. So you can't really be mad at me."

"Hmm." Locke nodded. "Technically, you sabotaged the bet. But I'm still paying you. I'm gentlemanly enough to do that."

Malik's eyelids lowered. His lips firmed. "You don't have to."

"Oh? And by the way. You're fired."

"You can't—"

"I can. I'm Eminent Master here and I sit on the board. At the head of the table. They will not defy me if I put it to a vote. So you can wait until it's official and public, or you can pack your things now and leave quietly."

New fury lit Malik's gaze. His mouth curled into a grimace. "You can't do that!"

"I just did."

Malik hissed, then threw Locke's tablet to the floor. It rattled on the tile, but did not break in its case.

The last Locke saw of him, he pounded the doorframe on his way out.

Silently, Locke turned toward the screens where Wulf paced.

Malik, whatever he had done, had damaged his slave. It explained why Wulf couldn't hear him every time he told him he had no intention of selling him. Wulf's trust had been hard won the first few days, but Malik's visit was a set-back. He believed everything before and after Malik was a trick for some cruel wager.

Locke had caught this error early enough to fix it. But it should never have happened in the first place.

As Locke watched, Wulf's pacing slowed. He approached the bed and sat.

Finally, he lifted his legs onto the bed and leaned back. When he reached for the remote to turn on the TV, something Locke had never seen him do on his own, Locke nodded.

"Good boy," he said. His slave was adjusting to his new environment.

Chapter Twenty - Wulf

Wulf started to rise from the bed as the door opened. In the waning afternoon light, he watched Locke enter. His heart beat in his throat. Locke's form, straight-lined, tall, with waves of brown hair about his ears and the back of his neck, drew him. Locke had mesmerized Wulf from the first time he had seen him. The man exuded an energy that Wulf's body instantly responded to.

The proof had happened only a short time ago in the alcove. Wulf wanted to stay at the Palace now. And if he was going to stay, he wanted it to be with Locke.

He muted the TV and set the remote at his side.

Locke held up his hand as Wulf started to climb out of the bed. "Stay."

Wulf scooted back, unsure, the covers pooling in his lap.

"I'm sorry I messed up," Wulf said.

He was not lying this time. Fear of doing wrong, or being cast out now that he had decided to stay was part of it, but now that he was more relaxed, he could finally admit to himself that his attraction to Locke, and his true desire to please the man — the master — prompted his apology.

"You did not mess up at all. But it is as if my words fall on deaf ears, Wulf. I told you about the lesson in trust. I then told you you did well."

Wulf lowered his head. It was hard for him to believe Locke because to Wulf's perception, he had lost control, he had messed the spread on the bed, and the feeling of loss within was just too strong.

Without another word, Locke came to the bed and sat on the edge. He bent.

Silently, Wulf watched him, and knew what he was doing though he could not see his hands. Locke was taking off his shoes.

Wulf had spent the past hour worrying about tricks and lies, but this man did not seem the type to resort to that. Eminent Master — that label meant something. It meant he'd earned the title. He had not lied or schemed or faked his way to it.

If Wulf could only get his emotional mind to believe his rational mind, he might be able to believe, to trust.

Everything Locke had told him indicated things were fine. Wulf was safe.

When Locke leaned back, lifting his legs onto the mattress, it was Wulf's turn to be surprised as Locke said, "I'm sorry you thought I was going to sell you."

"Malik told me —"

"I know," he interrupted. "I was unfair. I wasn't clear about you myself at first. That's my failure."

"I'll go back to the training room tomorrow. I promise I'll do better. I promise I'll —" Wulf's words left him as his throat closed up.

"We'll not go back to the training room again."

Wulf's heart fell. It was all a waste then, everything. He had failed, just as he had his whole life.

"No," Locke said, and his face was right near the side of Wulf's jaw. "Don't look like that. Don't. It's all right."

"I'm not going to get another chance?" Wulf asked shakily.

To Wulf's dismay, Locke smiled.

"I fired Malik."

Wulf leaned forward, looking intently into Locke's eyes.

Locke's smile dropped. He sighed. "Tell me, and please be honest. Did he touch you?"

Wulf gulped. "I am a slave. Does it matter?"

"You are my slave. Do you understand that? And it does matter to me that he hurt you."

"Is this why you won't take me back to the training room?"

"No." Locke took a deep breath, reached out to Wulf and touched him on the shoulder. "I only want to know if you are all right."

No one had ever asked Wulf such a question. Not when he was fighting and hurt, not when he felt bad, never. In Rille it was considered a weakness to admit to pain or emotional instability over any event. Even grief was shunted aside, allowed to manifest for perhaps a week at most. After that, it was back to life and work as usual.

"He did put his hands on me." Now Wulf's voice shook. "Here and here." He indicated his stomach, and his head. "He didn't physically hurt me until--." A long pause. "But he told me you were tricking me. That you wanted to earn my trust for the bet and then, when you won, you would sell me."

Slowly, Locke put his arm over Wulf's shoulders.

"And when you put your hands up to defend yourself from him?"

"He had attached the leash. I didn't know it. He yanked on it and—"

"I'm so sorry, Wulf. He's gone now. I sent him away. Can you believe me? Can you understand now that I have no intention of selling you?"

Wulf was quiet as he contemplated everything that had happened. It made sense that Malik would lie. Locke had a look in his eye Wulf could not deny. Open. Pensive. Unyielding in its longing. A hunger Wulf instinctively gravitated to.

"I want to believe you," Wulf said quietly.

"Then we will work on that. All right?"

Wulf frowned. "How? You just said you won't let me train."

186

"I only said we won't go back to the training room. We'll train here. Privately. There's simply no need to go to the public classes, the alcoves, the stage. You aren't to be sold. You're mine. Do you understand? You're mine."

"Train? Here?"

Locke's lashes made shadows on his cheeks as he closed his eyes halfway. "If you would have me."

What a strange way for a master to phrase his desire to a slave. "I? Have you?"

"Yes." Locke nodded. "That's exactly what I said."

"After everything you — you would — would want me?"

"I always have."

Locke smelled of rich spices from a foreign island, and warmth, almost sweet.

"But the question has been and always will be, do you want me?" Locke finished.

What was Locke asking?

"I am a slave. I signed consent forms. I don't get to have a choice," Wulf said.

"With me you do get a choice."

Wulf looked up into his face shadowed by the fall of his brown hair. But there was plenty of light in the room to see his dark eyes. Locke's eyes. Smiling at Wulf though his lips remained in a serious and straight line.

"Could you want me?" Locke asked again, voice so serious and low it vibrated all the way through Wulf's body.

"In my secret dreams and thoughts I do--," he gulped. "I have desired you."

Locke turned slightly so that their bodies faced each other.

"Really? It has not seemed obvious to me. I bought you because you combined everything I've wanted in a man. Strength. Ferocity. Beauty. Hopelessness. Even if you always hated me, I didn't care. I needed to save you."

"So it wasn't just starting with the bet?"

"No. It was before the bet. Malik saw my reaction to you in my face. He took that as an opportunity and made the wager. I was just drunk enough to accept. But that wasn't why I bought you."

Wulf realized if Locke had told him this days ago, even before Malik's visit, he could not have heard him. He could not have understood, but now the words meant everything to him.

"I'm curious. When did you start to notice — any attraction?" Locke asked.

"For you?" Wulf started to feel shy again.

Locke nodded. "Please. If what you say is true — "

"Since I fell off the stage." Wulf wanted to smile. It was hard. Those muscles hadn't worked for him in a long, long time. Smiling was for simpletons and children. But also, he knew deep inside in his heart that had hurt for so long, smiling was for lovers.

A warmth suffused Wulf's eyes.

"Then as my first training order to you, put your arms around me and see if that might feel all right."

He knew it would feel more than all right. It couldn't be otherwise. Locke was his master, but there had always been more. Wulf liked, in this moment, that Locke had given him an order. He quickened at the idea that he didn't have to worry that his actions and feelings might be wrong. The fact that Locke gave an order took his old inhibitions away and replaced them with a strange and wonderful yearning.

Wulf raised his arms. Up and out. He leaned into the warmth before he felt Locke's body against him, the black-shirted chest and arms.

He wasn't sure how to do this, whether he should put his arms under the other man's arms or over his shoulders. But instinct took over. He knew what he would like, how he would like to feel to have a man against him, in his arms. He wanted to push his way under Locke's arms, lower his head, touch his cheek to his neck.

His palms touched Locke's chest, feeling the silkiness of the shirt as he felt his way into an embrace. Locke seemed to adjust automatically as if knowing what Wulf wanted.

As Locke's arms came up and around him, Wulf inhaled the man's crisp mix of scents: spice from his skin, a fresh desert rain scent from deodorant perhaps, and soap from his newly laundered clothes.

Wulf wanted to breathe it in. Maybe forever.

"I want to lie here like this," Wulf whispered.

The TV still played on mute, flickering its light into the room, but Wulf did not see it. All he saw was black silk, skin, the side of a neck, the lobe of an ear, brown curls of shining hair. And lips in front of him. Smiling.

"That's all right. We can lie here like this all night."

Wulf felt the unused muscles in his face form his own smile again. Of course Locke would say that. From the beginning, he had said and done everything to better ease Wulf into every facet of his new and alien life. Why would Locke rush things now?

It seemed for hours they stayed like that.

He must have dozed off, for when he opened his eyes it was dark outside.

The city lights made the walls look burnished in blue and orange shadows. The TV had been turned off.

Locke was sitting up in the bed, fiddling with his tablet. Wulf lay curled against him, warm and at ease, his forehead butted up against the side of Locke's chest.

It was an odd thing for Wulf to enjoy this touch. To crave it. He'd never had this sort of closeness with another before, not even his parents. He didn't realize, until now, how starved he'd been.

Wulf sat up and swung his legs over the side of the bed. He had to pee.

Locke said nothing, but continued to fiddle with his tablet.

For some reason, Wulf no longer felt so naked in front of him. Maybe it was Locke's continuous calm demeanor. Maybe it was how he spoke to Wulf, not as a lewd master like Malik was, but respectful, with genuine care.

When Wulf came out of the bathroom, a steaming tray of food sat at the foot of the bed taking up almost the entire space.

Locke was quietly serving up potato salad and green beans onto plates holding what looked like turkey sandwiches. He handed him a plate.

Wulf started to take it and move to the chairs.

"No. Stay here. Just relax."

"And eat in the bed?" Wulf asked cautiously.

"Yes."

Wulf put a napkin in his lap and leaned back with the plate of food. It felt both decadent and provocative to have a meal in bed when he was not sick anymore.

Locke put the TV on, but Wulf could not remember what they watched. Only that the food tasted wonderful, and that this haven of security and warmth which he was not used to included Locke.

When they finished, Locke used his tablet to ring a slave to come take the dishes and tray away.

The TV droned, but all Wulf could hear was the gentle breathing of the man beside him, and feel the warmth. He no longer wrestled with such a sense of shame. The new sensations of acceptance, safety and caring thrummed through him, obscuring all else.

The idea that he could be well-fed, well taken care of, and never face hunger or cold or homelessness or a prison of iron bars amazed him. How heavy and tight his heart had been his whole life. This moment—the confessions, the nap and the meal—had opened him after he'd lived closed off in fear and hate for so long.

Locke's presence infiltrated everything—Wulf's pores, his thoughts, his blood. Sitting next to him now, quiet, allowing his mind the freedom to wander, made his blood begin to burn.

And he began to think thoughts he never imagined he would willingly think, especially after such a short time at the Palace.

Please let Locke put his arm around me again.

I want another massage.

Will Locke allow me to learn to give a massage in return?

What will it feel like to have his lips against mine… or on my cock?

What will it feel like to have him take me, be inside me, holding me, moving back and forth?

The capacity of the human body to feel so much so fast astounded him. His skin went from normal to hot in a matter of seconds. His thoughts alone enflamed him.

The sheet, blanket and spread of the bed rested on his knees and thighs, covering him just enough to hide his arousal. Thankfully. It was like dealing with a restless fever, this sensation of desire, this waiting for yet another touch from the powerful man beside him.

Wulf's knees bent of their own will. The soles of his feet rubbed the bed sheet, dislodging the covers. Every breath he took seemed deeper, deeper. As if he could not get enough oxygen. His mind floated away on euphoric hopes and he could not explain it, and didn't want to.

The room, the TV, everything diminished until all that he knew to be real from one moment to the next was Locke and himself, side by side, breathing, being in a weird sense of togetherness.

Locke said in his habitual quiet voice, "I can turn it off."

"What?" Wulf's mind fogged on the statement.

"The TV."

"Yes," Wulf replied. Silence would be better.

He didn't know if something was wrong with him anymore. He couldn't think. Rille was so far behind him in such a short time that it was still a shock to his system. He didn't need to fight anymore. He didn't need to plow into unseen enemy lines because it was right and for no other reason, personal or otherwise, without regard to his own well-being.

But duty had called him all his life. He needed—no, *wanted*—to obey something or someone with mindless abandon. He was good at that. Thinking too much hurt him more than a punch to the gut or the graze of a bullet. More, even, than his collar set on high.

And then there was his body, so hot and liquid in ways he'd never abandoned himself to. The scorching anticipation of something, his skin melting for it. For a touch. For Locke.

"Yes," Wulf said again. The TV was off and he didn't know what question he was answering now.

Locke turned to him. Gaze penetrating. Filling Wulf with more than just a look, but with his presence, with a possible *future*.

The back of Wulf's throat clenched and a small gush of air escaped him like a soft sound he had no control over.

"There are only three things I will ever ask of you as my slave," Locke said.

Three things? Wulf wanted to hear what they were. But the way the muscles of Locke's lips moved around the vowel sounds of the words, and the tiny bit of moisture glistening against his white teeth had Wulf drowning in a desire he couldn't push away. Pink. Lips. And the shadow of a tongue.

Wulf shivered and tried to concentrate.

"Honesty. You must always tell me the truth when I ask you a question."

The words muffled again. Wulf tried to concentrate but his cock and his balls were heavier than words, shouting with a strain of need.

"...obedience. I will ask your opinion on things, but I require..."

192

Those words were lost, too. Obedience, did he say? Wulf didn't care. He'd learn it later. Locke would be giving him private lessons from now on. There was lots of time.

"…the third, trust in me. You cannot do the first two without trust. Trust is something more difficult than…"

The sentence faded away but the lips still moved. Wulf watched that mouth, then moved his gaze to the throat where the skin was tanned and tight over the Adam's apple and then lower, to the buttons of Locke's black shirt.

Those buttons strained against a strong chest, strong enough to be a force for Wulf's needs. His eyes darted lower to the flat stomach, the thighs, the bulge between. To press, push... What was he thinking?

"…understand?"

Wulf blinked, and lifted his eyes. Locke had asked him a question.

He found himself nodding although it was for his own purpose, for what he wanted now. Locke's three things? Not an issue.

Not now.

He wanted to kiss the man. And in this room, here in the Slave Palace, apparently it wasn't a sin but a goal to be achieved. An act of pleasure wrapped in roles but given like a gift.

But Wulf didn't want to kiss Locke because he was the slave. He wanted to kiss him because Locke was Locke. And he wanted him. And if it was a gift to pursue the act, it was also a selfish gesture. For he wanted to feel it like a waking, like a blush of morning sun.

He'd had so little of blushing and suns and selfishness in his life.

Locke started to speak again.

Wulf leaned in, then, not caring. The collar tugged at his neck. He didn't mind it anymore. This was worth the risk, worth another kind of fight. His body ached as if to say, *Please.*

Locke's eyes widened, a dark but accepting shock within, and that was all Wulf saw before he was too close, before he smashed his lips to the other man's mouth.

It wasn't a shy first kiss for him. But a rough taking, his mouth open and demanding before he could think, understand, or feel any shame. He was free for once, and he was going to embrace the lost-and-found essence of it.

Wulf's hands came up. He wasn't conscious and yet he was more conscious than ever of all the things he wanted now, the way he felt and the way he wanted more.

His fingers clenched tight to Locke's upper arms, feeling the silk of his shirt scrape against his nails, the hard muscles underneath.

If Locke pushed him away now, he had an idea that he would just grab again and again until the man stopped, until he grew tired and languid and accepting.

But that didn't happen. Locke was like a wall he was trying to climb, unyielding and hard with slippery surfaces where purchase was hard to obtain, but that wall turned to more level surfaces with dips and crevices.

He felt Locke's chest move as he gasped against Wulf's mouth, and then the arms of his master came up and around him, a gentle pressure of hands on the backs of his shoulders.

He was held. He was held and it was better than anything, better than food, a comfortable bed, or a well-oiled massage. Better than the best the world had never offered him.

To be held. Embraced. Accepted.

He felt his body come up from the bed and his knees go under him as he pushed himself further against Locke, clutching, kissing deeply now, tongue invading. To his amazement Locke went with him, toppling back, letting Wulf come over him, straddle him, press his entire naked length to him.

194

Wulf was surprised that Locke let him. Then he wasn't. For Locke had wanted him to embrace himself fully on this level, and that was exactly what he was doing.

Locke's mouth opened easily to him, relaxed and silken, and he tasted of the autumn outdoors, rich and wine-fed. Wulf wanted to engulf him.

He was bigger than Locke, more heavily muscled, so he worried he might press too hard, or shove an elbow or knee where it wasn't desired. But Locke seemed not to care, for his arms moved tighter about Wulf's back, squeezing.

He couldn't breathe. He didn't want to. He wanted more of this.

One of Locke's hands curved up until it rested alongside Wulf's face, the fingers digging into his hair. He leaned into that touch, pulling back only enough for a breath, then diving in again.

Locke turned his head and his hot breath dusted Wulf's cheek, making Wulf's whole face burn. Wulf made low noises in his throat, seeking more flavors and textures. He wanted, no, *needed* to be filled up with sensation.

His mouth kissed the rough jaw-line where Locke's evening shadow of a beard had started to appear. He let his tongue trace the spiced skin, feel the prickle of the hard hairs, and it fueled him as his mouth moved downward to the side of Locke's neck.

Wulf's skin sizzled all over, but his cock was the hottest of all flames, a thing of pure hard need pulsing against the front of Locke's trousers. Locke's hand tore through Wulf's hair until it cupped the back of his neck, and held him hard as Wulf sucked at the skin just below the jaw.

He shouldn't have known what he was doing. But he knew. What he'd seen the others doing as he glimpsed them in the training room, or on the video he could not finish watching which had spurred him whether he'd wanted it to or not.

It wasn't as if he didn't know about sex and lust and the forbidden physical things men might do to each other. He did know from what children talked about, and what he'd picked up on the streets. And even from the careful classroom teachings on what was never ever done.

You tell a child they can't think of something because it is bad and they can't help but think about it. Learn about it. It was how he knew he was gay. Simply, he had never been in a situation of unchecked desire. The knowledge lay dormant in him until now.

Warm air in his ear. A whisper. "So. This."

Locke lifted his head up; Wulf's mouth felt swollen, stinging just a little where Locke's beard had pricked. He gulped. He kissed Locke lighter on the lips, close-mouthed this time, and pulled back so he could look into his eyes.

Locke whispered close to his lips, "Our first real training session? Yes?"

Wulf frowned at him. His breaths came fast, as if he were on the verge of sobbing. But it was ecstasy, not pain he felt. Not fear.

"I don't want to train right now. I want to feel more. More of what happened this afternoon."

Locke's cheeks plumped with his smile. "Then feel. I give myself freely to you. Whatever you wish."

Whatever Wulf wished? A thrill washed through his body. He almost came from those simple words. The excitement made his lips stretch over his teeth. He wanted to moan, groan, maybe yell or howl. He was so uncontained in his wants, his craving for Locke. All of him, body, heart, words.

What would it feel like? The heat of this man, the thrill, his tongue his mouth his hips his hands his cock inside him plunging jamming touching so deep?

Air gusted from his lungs. Locke's smile turned to a grin and both his hands came up and framed Wulf's face.

Wulf lunged for the kiss before Locke could take any control. His hands came between them and fumbled for the buttons of Locke's thin black shirt.

Finally, Locke caught a breath and said, "Priceless. You are priceless. Sweet angel, do not wait any longer."

He put his hands on his own shirt and helped to undo it, leaning up and shrugging out of it as Wulf attacked his belt, his zipper. Everything got taken off, pulled away, thrown to the floor in rustling heaps. Shirt. Shoes. Socks.

When Wulf pulled at the dark trousers, Locke lifted himself and allowed the touch.

Wulf's fingernails scraped a taut waist and firm buttocks as he tugged, revealing more beautiful flesh light-toasted brown, the muscles ridged and corded now with the tension of his desire.

The hipbones made beautiful rises on the skin, and it dented so perfectly on either side, the beginnings of a V, which would bottom out at the groin.

Locke stayed taut but motionless as Wulf slid the trousers all the way, taking the underwear with them, yanking them off the feet one at a time, then tossing them hard to the floor.

He wanted to burn this image into his eyes. How Locke lay back against the blue pillows fully aroused, his cock curved up toward his belly, the tip glimmering with sweet excitement.

The musk of arousal was salty, ocean-sweet. Fascinated, Wulf dove for the stomach, licking, tasting the salt, then moving his head lower. He had to brush the tip of that cock. His tongue yearned.

And then he was doing it, licking Locke where he never thought he'd ever lick another man. So forbidden. Against the law. A prison-bound offense.

Lovely. So much like salted wine. An essence of something that sent shivers through Wulf's body as he tasted and wanted more, wanted to drink.

He was all animal now, sniffing, backing off because he wanted to see. More and more. He touched Locke's cock, took it in his hand to feel the smoothness, the hardness, how it pulsed in his grip.

Voice low and thick, Wulf heard himself. "I want to see."

He couldn't get enough. Now he licked the underside of the cock as he let it go and it smacked the flat abdomen. Hands on Locke's hips, he said gruffly, "I want to see," even as he was turning Locke.

Locke relaxed, eyelids half closed, hands behind his head as if ready to sleep, as if hypnotized by this pure lust, rolled to accommodate.

Locke's buttocks were hard and round, but soft and warm to the touch with tiny pale hairs all over, pure maleness, pure elegance better even than the painted live sculptures outside.

Wulf's hands were on them, palms pressing, fingers squeezing, wrenching them apart to even hotter skin, to dark swirls of hair and a pucker, an opening, a mouth of darkness inviting. He lowered his head. He inhaled. He poked.

Locke gave a small, muffled laugh. "There's oil in the drawer."

"What?"

Locke would allow this?

"Take what you want. Use me. Examine me. Get your fill."

"But—you, I want you in me," Wulf said, kneeling up, letting Locke roll again on the bed until their eyes could meet. "I want to know. I want to know everything!"

Locke leaned up on his elbow. So nakedly exquisite— dark pink nipples erect, the ripple of ribs, the curlicue of the navel—that Wulf almost choked on the sensations that pulsed through him.

"I guarantee that will happen." Locke's dark brows hunched low, eyes flashing.

Wulf's cock bobbed. His balls were so full he could not imagine they weren't huge and ready to explode.

Locke reached across more pillows, one knee bending, rocking forward, and opened a drawer by the bedside. He withdrew and waved a vial of oil.

"Use this. And touch me all you wish."

Wulf grabbed for it, balancing with one hand on Locke's hip. Their hands met and Locke wove his fingers with Wulf's. The vial was trapped between their palms now, their gazes twined.

Locke slid his hand away and Wulf gripped the bottle. He opened it and poured the liquid into his palm and slid it, without warning, up and down Locke's erect cock.

A hiss came from his master.

Wulf stroked up again, thumbing the tip where he longed to place his mouth, then down and around the balls, cupping them. Further back, he explored and Locke opened his legs, slid up in the bed and grabbed a pillow.

Locke shoved it under his backside, raising his hips up and giving Wulf access to his pucker. Wulf probed, liking the way the muscle stretched around his finger, amazed at the heat there, the tightness, and though he'd known about this sort of contact, and seen it in the training room and videos, he grew concerned that an erect cock—especially one of his size—would not fit.

But what he really wanted right now was to continue to look and touch.

He glanced up and saw Locke was back to his half-lidded, hypnotized demeanor.

Locke raised an eyebrow at him and said one word. "Deeper."

Wulf pushed his finger past the tight muscle to slippery softness. Locke moaned and seemed to like it, so he slid it in further, then in and out stroking gently.

"Tilt your finger up. There's a bump. It's a gland and it gives such pleasure."

Wulf obeyed, finding the spot, and Locke drew in a fast breath. "Yes!" His cock twitched.

Locke's body gave off a deep bronze sheen as it glowed. Everything became slick and warm and smooth between them.

When Wulf removed his finger, Locke let out a moan that was almost disappointment, but not for long as Wulf bent forward to kiss him again. Locke's hands stroked Wulf's chest, fingertips running over hard muscle and peaked nipples.

He wanted to feel all of Locke against him and couldn't stop the movement of his hips against Locke's and more surges of heat as their cocks pressed together against taut abdomens.

Locke pushed Wulf to his side until they were facing each other.

Wulf said, "Don't make me stop."

"I won't." Locke ran a hand alongside his head. "But I want to touch you and pet you, too. Taste you."

A tremble ran through Wulf, hot and liquid.

"You're so eager and young, so hard. I want to make you come. It won't be like earlier today. It won't be an accident. It will be because we want this. You can relax and let go. Just feel. Once that happens, then we can continue, take our time."

"What do I do?"

"Lie back."

Pillows cushioned Wulf's shoulders and head. He wanted this more than he had ever allowed himself to acknowledge. His ejaculation from the massage had happened too quickly and shame had overcome the pleasure, though he could still recall the sensation well enough to know he wanted to repeat it, do it right.

When Locke ran his hands over Wulf's chest again, he could not keep from arching his back. Wulf's cock pointed heavy and hard to his bellybutton. It rose and fell with his

200

jerking motion, clear liquid beading at the tip, which protruded round and pink from his foreskin.

Locke kissed him again on the lips, but this time it was quick. Wulf missed that mouth when it left his, that pressure, that wonderful salt-sweet taste.

But soon he forgot the loss as Locke's lips and tongue kissed and licked his throat, then trailed over his chest. Hands ran down his sides as lips found Wulf's left nipple and gave a pull.

Wulf cried out in pleasure. It was so much, almost too much. His body couldn't stay still though he tried to relax.

When that nipple was thoroughly explored, Locke found the other, doing the same to it. Wulf's whole body felt ready to explode.

Slowly, Locke worked his way down Wulf's torso, licking, kissing. He crawled between his legs and his hands ran down Wulf's inner thighs, leaving trails of fire. Wulf's balls tensed. He was going to come.

"Not yet," Locke said, as if he could read and feel Wulf's responses through body language. Their connection was growing stronger. Wulf didn't need to ask for anything.

Locke put his palm against Wulf's groin, forefinger and thumb circling the base of his cock, which perked even more, standing straight up now. The pressure eased the immediate feeling of impending orgasm, and Wulf could take a deeper breath—only to expel it all as he felt Locke's mouth encase the head of his cock.

He could not help but kick out with one leg. His hands fisted the bedspread. He let out a strange sound, like a sob and an exclamation of astonished dismay at the same time.

When Locke began to suck, Wulf thrust up with his hips without meaning to. He wanted to relax, but those lips, that mouth—and now it was sinking down on him in such exquisite glory that even his deepest most forbidden desires had never imagined it could be this good.

Such burning. Such a roaring within. Surely he was moving too high too fast. He was going to come apart. He was going to fly up into a million pieces that would become forever lost in infinity.

He wanted this to last. His body struggled with itself to hold onto this pleasure and not let go too soon. He started to mumble words that made no sense as the mouth moved over his shaft up and down.

As it came up, the tongue tickled the head of his cock in such a way that he could feel the warm liquid begin to bubble through him, though he was still holding on, still gripping the spread and curling his toes trying to prolong some semblance of control.

This was amazing. But Locke had said to relax into it, that they would continue on through the night. This wasn't an ending, but a beginning.

Wulf thought he would like to do this all night, if possible.

The mouth did amazing things to him, sometimes rising all the way off and dipping to lick at his balls, other times taking him all the way down until he could feel the tip of his cock jut against the roof of Locke's mouth, then slide into the softness of the throat.

The sucking got him so wet and then there was thrusting again. He couldn't stop, back and forth, the mouth taking him in, the pull and the wiggle of the tongue driving him into a white frenzy.

His words, which seemed incoherent, became coherent again only because he was begging for it. Clutching the bedspread as if it might ground him.

"Please. Yes. I can't hold back. I'm going to—I'm going to—"

Locke sucked harder and the peak of brightness went golden. He was coming fast and hard, so hard his teeth knocked together and his throat closed. All breath froze in his lungs. His body went rigid. Everything he could never have now felt like it was pouring over him, all the pleasure of the world and beyond, for all time.

Somewhere in the room a man was moaning over and over, loud enough to be heard amidst the drowning howling of his body in ecstasy.

His cock spasmed and jerked again and again as Locke sucked all he had to give.

Slowly, gently he wafted on his euphoria. Even as his cock left that hot, wonderful mouth, he still floated. Arms went around him, pulled him against a hard chest.

Words. Buoyant and yet grounding. Patient and caring. Loving. "Yes. That's it. My love, you are beautiful, beautiful."

He was panting against a slick chest, smooth as satin, hard muscles rippling beneath soft skin. His cheek pressed and then he was rubbing his whole face there, breathing in, and pressing into Locke's neck inhaling rich scents of passion: spice, musk, the smokiness of hot skin.

Hands smooth his hair back from his face, cupped his cheeks, kissed him hard. Wulf tasted himself, tart and earthy, cloying. He opened his mouth wide and allowed Locke to plunder it.

His hands automatically ran down Locke's belly, over a hip, encountering a hard cock. He wrapped his fingers around it just to feel and it jerked and pulsed. He pulled back, looking down.

Locke was coming and white streams jetted from the tip of his handsome shaft.

Wulf squeezed and pulled up. More white spray shot, then eased, still fountaining out and over the pink head.

"Look what you did to me," Locke said quietly.

"I—" Wulf glanced up to see Locke smiling, not disappointed. Anything but.

"I usually need more stimulation," Locke said. "But I guess with you that's all out the window."

Wulf tilted his head. "Really?"

Locke let out a short laugh.

Wulf continued to pet Locke's still half-hard cock, wanting to savor the texture, remembering how it tasted when he'd licked it, wanting to taste it again... soon.

They tumbled on the bed together, Locke laughing, Wulf just trying to catch his breath. This was all so new and wonderful. He wanted more. He couldn't quite relax yet, but he would find his way.

Hands went everywhere. Mouths met. Bodies undulated against each other, sliding on sweat and semen and oil. The bed and pillows encased them. The room grew steamy.

Tongues licked hard nipples and burgeoning cocks. Fingers probed, oiled and smooth.

Wulf was hard in no time, yet it felt less urgent but still impossibly good.

When Locke was fully erect again, he pushed himself between Wulf's widespread legs, rubbing against his balls and the crack of his ass. He leaned down and sucked on the tip of Wulf's cock, then backed up on his knees and pushed against the backs of Wulf's thighs.

He'd been playing with him, opening him up for what seemed like hours. Now Wulf was ready. He wanted this. He wanted to feel filled to brim until he could not breathe again, flying so high he'd never come all the way back to Earth, a part of him left to wander the stars.

"Yes," Wulf said.

Locke leaned into him, chest to chest, holding his cock in position but not moving. He kissed Wulf's lips lightly, then said, "A consent form is one thing. But this means more. Tell me *yes* one more time and it will be so."

"Yes. Please. I want you. I want you."

Locke reached between them and rubbed his cock against Wulf's hole. His dark eyes gazed into Wulf's as he slid forward, so smooth, the path well-oiled and ready. His muscles were relaxed and gave easily after the first wince and burn.

204

Locke slid in the rest of the way easily and now they were truly connected, merged.

Wulf tossed his head back on the pillow and moaned. He was so full. Brimming and flying, just as he'd wished for.

Slowly, Locke began to move. Everything seemed glistening and wet—the lights against the windows, the very air of the room itself.

He reached up and gripped Locke's shoulders, hanging on for dear life.

This was too good. This was not what he thought would happen to him when he was first caught and imprisoned and then labeled a One-Night Thrall.

"Locke," he said between breaths. "Locke, don't let go. Please don't let go of me. I want—I want—"

And he was soaring. The rhythm increased and inside and out he was trembling, on fire, his cock rising, so hard, so hard. Locke reached between them and wrapped his fingers around Wulf's shaft and that was all he needed, just that touch and he was spurting.

All thought wiped out of his mind. He could still feel the cock inside him pushing into him, pressing a special place that sent volcanic eruptions throughout his body, but no thoughts. Just feeling. And more feeling. His breath locked up again, his throat and chest tight.

Locke groaned and said, "I've never felt this way before. It's as if you own me and not me who owns you."

Wulf thrilled at the words.

Locke continued to murmur, seemed unable to stop. "Oh, you are gripping me so tight. I'm coming. Oh, yes, you are so sweet, so sweet—"

Locke fell on top of Wulf, still hard, still inside him even as the pulsings slowed, then stopped.

Their arms locked around each other.

"I won't let you go," Locke said. "Ever."

Wulf looked up at him. Into the dark infinity of his master's gaze. "I believe you now."

Their lips met again. And again, they were lost.

Epilogue - Locke

Locke helped Wulf to step up and onto the marble pedestal. Gleaming and golden, his slave nearly eclipsed the sun.

Wulf held his head high. His broad shoulders jutted back, showing off the remarkable pecs, every inch of his naked form painted in shades of ochre, fawn, amber, gold.

Wulf's erect cock stood straight out and proud. He had no trouble maintaining it, young as he was, as long as Locke was around to admire him. Wulf responded to that admiration more and more every day.

Locke gazed at him. The most splendid man, the most generously needy and beautiful soul he'd ever met. When Wulf wasn't in Locke's arms, they ached. Locke could not get enough of him. He licked his lips, letting his gaze wander up and down that gorgeous body.

Wulf's cock jerked in response. Just that — Locke's unconditional admiration and love — made his slave hard. He barely had to touch him to make him come sometimes.

"I will be here walking the grounds, not far off. Think of me watching you from vantages where you cannot see me. I'll bring you down for a brief break in an hour. Then you can go back up if you want. We can do this all afternoon."

"I'd like that so much," Wulf replied. His voice was so different now, much more confident than when Locke had first met him. There were no tremors, no hidden angers, no subtle hints of rage, disgust, fear or denial anymore.

Locke had gotten lucky with this one. He'd opened him up with the right key at the right moment and the man — the pure art and essence of what he was — had become his.

He hoped it would stay that way forever.

The End

Dear Reader:

Thank you for reading my fantasy romance *The Slave Palace*.

Please consider leaving a review. Word of mouth is like gold! If it weren't for the generous support of my readers, I could not be writing more books!

If you enjoyed this book, you might also enjoy subscribing to my newsletter. I put it out several times a year to announce new books and upcoming projects, and I always have sales and freebies to offer readers both from myself and other authors I enjoy reading. If you subscribe at the link below, you can get a free copy of my contemporary mm romance "Buying You."

Or, if newsletters aren't your thing, it is very easy to sign up for my Facebook group Wendyland to keep up to date.

For new release notifications, it's super easy to just follow my author page on Amazon.

I have more upcoming standalone books in my Kingdom of Slaves series.

The Slave Harem.

The Secret Slave.

Release dates for both: Spring, 2019!

Happy Reading!

Contact links for Wendy Rathbone:

Join my Facebook group Wendyland:
https://www.facebook.com/groups/718074255203918/

Facebook: https://www.facebook.com/wendy.rathbone.3

Newsletter sign up (you get a free copy of my contemporary mm romance "Buying You"):
https://claims.prolificworks.com/free/iE2sKi9b

Amazon author page: https://www.amazon.com/Wendy-Rathbone/e/B00B0O9BMS/ref=dp_byline_cont_ebooks_1

About Wendy Rathbone

I love to write.

The reason I write romance these days is because the overwhelming power of falling in love (which has been proven to heal even cancer) is a game-changer. It makes sad people instantly happy. It makes bleak reality look sun-warmed and friendly again.

I have written in all genres: scifi, fantasy, horror, paranormal, contemporary, erotica, romance. But I keep coming back to romance. Gay romance. Male/male romance. The idea of two men falling in love in a society that has winced at that sort of thing for far too long is alluring. Many of my themes involve abduction, pleasure slavery, indentured servitude, and imprisonment. It's like, with my writing, I'm constantly breaking out of some self-imposed cage and letting my wings unfurl until I can finally fly. I also love mismatched couples.

This is why I write. This is what makes me burn.

All my books are available on Amazon and most are in Kindle Unlimited. So if you have the urge, go take a look. See what's on the shelf.

Love to you all!

Wendy Rathbone

LORD VAMPYRE
Wendy Rathbone

When Lord Neverelle becomes a guest at Cliffside Keep, Vanni watches helplessly as Damion, the young man he's grown up with and secretly loves, falls for the alluring and seductive stranger. Lord Neverelle is danger incarnate, and soon takes control of the household.

Not satisfied with Damion alone, Never uses a vampire trick called "the tempt" to compel Vanni, who is swept into a love triangle that includes fiery passion and nightly threesomes.

Now Vanni must ask himself, is any of this consensual? And what about Damion—does he really want to be with Vanni, or is it all a sensual play controlled by vampire compulsion?

M/M and M/M/M romance.

Also available in paperback, on Amazon, or order from your favorite bookseller.

THE IMPOSTER KING
(Book 2 of The Imposter Series)
Wendy Rathbone

Their love made them close. Their secret kept them closer.

Dare and Prince Malory are happily married and in love, but the secret of Dare's true identity as a mere servant threatens their romantic bliss.

Messages to the king of Brookfall go unanswered, and rumors of war unsettle both kingdoms. Until one day heralds arrive with bags of gold to ransom Dare and demand his return to Brookfall.

King Millard, Prince Malory's father, orders Dare to make the journey to see his father. But Dare is not the true heir, and if they meet, the secret he and Mal have been guarding will be revealed. Also, impersonating a royal means a death penalty offense. Worse, it could mean all-out war between their countries.

Panic. Despair. Lovers torn asunder. Personal sacrifice. More dark secrets revealed. An ending that will leave you breathless.

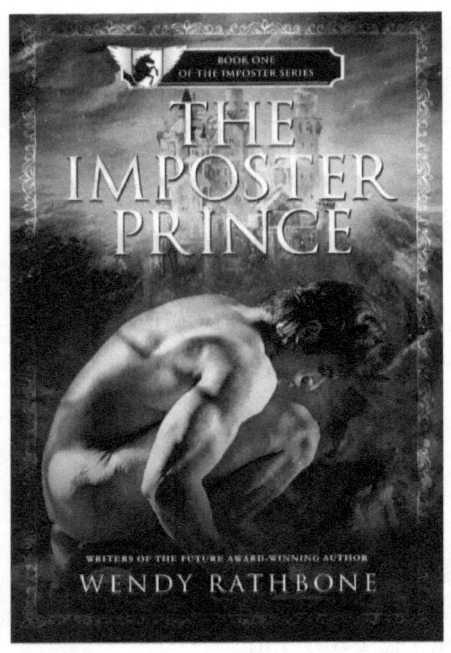

The Imposter Prince
Book 1 in The Imposter Series
Wendy Rathbone

His love for an enemy prince threatens his very life.

Dare does not mind serving the spoiled and cruel Prince Darius. Growing up with him, Dare does everything for Darius including homework, bed play demands, and even doubling for him as the prince grows too paranoid to face even the smallest of crowds.

But everything changes in a single moment when Dare, while posing as Darius, is abducted by the enemy.

A captive in a new and hostile land, Dare meets another prince who seems just as indulged and rotten as Darius—until Dare gets to know him, until they fall in love. Against his will, Dare must continue to play the role of Prince Darius for real, or risk everything: his love, his land, and his very life.

His only chance for survival is to keep a secret from the one he loves, a secret that is also killing him.

A male/male, enemies to lovers novel of mad kings, troubled princes, abduction, fevers, cold dungeons, warm hearths, comfort, wine, and true love.

The Imposter Prince

Also available in paperback on Amazon, or order from your favorite bookseller.

214

Ganymede: Abducted by the Gods
Book 1 in "The Fantastic Immortals" Series
Wendy Rathbone

My name is Ganymede, and I have been betrayed.

Every boy my age dreams of leaving home to embark on a noble adventure, but never does any boy imagine it happening as it did to me. On the evening of my 18th naming day, when I expected no more than a chalice of wine and a few drunken flirtations to tempt my innocence, I was instead sold by my father to the god, Zeus - not because of anything particular I had ever done or said, but solely because I am considered beautiful among mortals, and my father found more value in a few gold coins than in the well-being of his youngest son.

To be honest, I never believed in the gods, but my lack of belief held no power in Olympus or on Earth. Now under Zeus's influence, I am kept drunk on ambrosia in the sun-lit halls of the immortals, alternately amazed and horrified at the power these beings hold over others, and how darkly they influence the progress of humanity itself. How very much I want to hate Zeus for kidnapping me, and yet he shows me mostly kindness, even on that fateful night when we shared a bed for the first time. Kindness, yes, but also a godly and unyielding refusal to take no for an answer... probably because he could read my ambrosia-fevered curiosity as much as my naive, inexperienced terror. He owns me, after all, just as he owns everything else, so perhaps it never occurred to him that a captive and a slave might not make the best of lovers.

Throughout my time at Olympus - who's to say how long I've been here, for time on Olympus is not the same as that on Earth - the only thing that gives me hope comes to me in dreams and visions. His name is Sable and he is a magnificent shape-shifter in the form of a giant raven. When he first spoke to me in my mind it was with a resonance unlike any I had ever known - his mind and mine sounding a single note together, a song without words, a promise of freedom, a glimpse of some distant but very real possibility of this thing we humans call Love. But now he is silent. Perhaps I dreamed his voice. Perhaps I have finally lost my mind...

The sequel to "Ganymede" is entitled...
Zeus: Conquering His Heart (Book 2 in "The Fantastic Immortals" Series

Both books in "The Fantastic Immortals" Series are also available in paperback on Amazon, or order from your favorite bookseller.

ZEUS (Conquering His Heart)
Book 2 in "The Fantastic Immortals" Series
WENDY RATHBONE

When I throw the lightning and summon the thunder, it isn't always out of anger, but often from a love so all-consuming it could only be the effect of Eros himself. Yes, he is beautiful. Of course he is. How could he be otherwise, with hair the color of sunlight and white-feathered wings that drape to the floor? And he is as ancient as the myth of time itself, an immortal with powers and glamour beyond my ability to imagine. He struggles to teach me wisdom, control, strategy, yet I sit here babbling like a child, for all I can think of is how I might try - at least let me try! - to prove myself to him in some way that will cause him to crave my company and my touch, just as I crave his.

I do not yet know how to be a god, for I am only 18 and still just a silly boy who has fallen in love with Love himself, while my father Cronus plots and schemes to lock me in his dungeon and make me his slave forever.

A male/male romance.

Also available in paperback on Amazon, or order from your favorite bookseller.

Wendy Rathbone

PREY
Wendy Rathbone

When the rescued slaves were first brought on board my ship, I saw only the one. The one they called Arcana. And though I realized the others had all suffered similar fates - fearsome torture and erotic conditioning that had estranged them from whoever they had once been - I focused on the one who met my eyes with what could only be interpreted as a defiantly seductive lure, while the others held their gazes downward, at their feet, at the floor, at the past which had shaped them and undoubtedly doomed them to any sort of normal life.

Not so with Arcana. That one had no shame in whatever had happened to him. In that one blinding moment when we saw one another for the first time, I knew he was as brash as he was beautiful, and I knew without any doubt that he had chosen me - though for what dark agenda, I could not have said.

My heart went cold and silent in my chest. My throat was dry. My breathing faltered and I was forever changed.

***

We danced. Captain Mordecai and I. Not any traditional dance, but a dance of power. A battle of yin and yang, light and dark, pleasure and torment. A dangerous dance of right and wrong in a single moment caught outside the tendrils of Time.

It was easy to see the raw and sensual power in that man's gaze. But also the fear. Fear of being seen for who he was behind his carefully-constructed masks. Fear of finally surrendering to the dangerous desires he clearly felt when he looked at me, knowing my past, knowing I had been enslaved by sadistic aliens. Knowing I had not only enjoyed it, but had come to love my master. All the wrong things. So very wrong.

That was when I knew he wanted me. That was when I knew I needed him.

That was when I knew I had him exactly where we both needed him to be.

Also available in paperback on Amazon,
or order from your favorite bookseller.

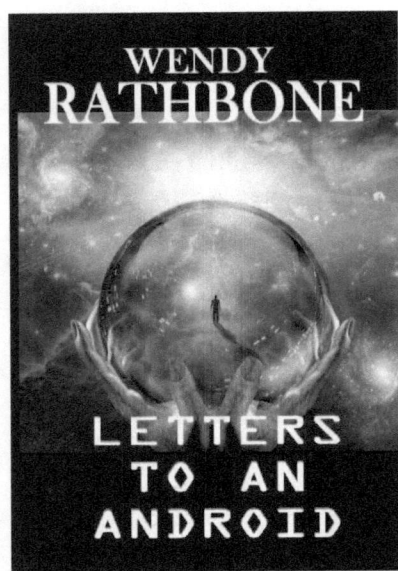

LETTERS TO AN ANDROID
Wendy Rathbone

Cobalt is a created human, vat grown and born adult, with no human rights and indentured to serve others for the duration of his life. Liyan is a young man with wanderlust in his eyes, embarking on a career that takes him to the furthest regions of space. The two become unlikely friends and create a memorable long-distance correspondence. Through Liyan, Cobalt gets to explore the universe, living vicariously through his friend's wave transmissions. A strong bond develops between them that not even the stars can put asunder.

Now you know an android who writes poetry.

This is all your fault. Did you not read my last wave telling you extracurricular activities for my kind are discouraged? Of course this is harmless and strangely enjoyable and does not necessarily require me to leave the hotel. Pel would not care if I wrote lines of equations or nonsensical juxtaposed words. As long as the act does not bring my mental state into question.

However, in history, poetry is often written by the rebels.

So we can keep this to ourselves.

Let me know about your lieutenant's test.

And to give you peace of mind, I never believed you observed me as anything other than human.

Some people are and always will be hateful bigots. Most people are simply uncomfortable in speaking to "property." And anyway, friendship, like poetry, is also discouraged.

Your friend,

Cobalt

Also available in paperback on Amazon, or order from your favorite bookseller.

SCOUNDREL
Wendy Rathbone

Antares is a willing sex slave, trained in the harems of Anada since the age of 18, and owned by a wealthy master who spoils his slaves. But all that changes when Empire soldiers invade Antares' world and he is taken away from the only life he's ever known.

In a colonized galaxy where starships are as common as houseflies, and a dark Empire seeks to control thousands of civilized worlds, there are those who fall through the cracks and refuse to be conquered, including the pirate, Slate, and his crew.

Out in the darkness of the unknown, among Empire soldiers and scoundrels, will bad fates befall Antares and his fellow captive companions?

Will Slate finally find the love he's been looking for his whole life?

Can Slate and Antares ever see eye to eye?

A male/male romance to end all male/male romances!

LACE
Wendy Rathbone

Lace is a being from another dimension on Earth. He cannot die and humans call his kind "vampire" and declare war on them.

Firi is a human military soldier, a trained guard, who has met Lace twice in his young life and formed a bond with him.

In a world where humans and vampires are arch enemies, where vampires are eradicated in horrible ways, where being a vampire-lover means a death sentence, can Firi and Lace ever find each other again and explore the feelings they have for each other?

Will Lace be able escape his government prison, and the amnesia that keeps him from accessing his true powers?

Can Firi, the boy he met in the woods ten years ago, ever hope to help him?

A male/male romance about secrets that can get you killed, impossible rescues, and old lovers who cannot be trusted.

Also available in paperback on Amazon,
or order from your favorite bookseller.

220

SONS OF NEVERLAND
Della Van Hise

"The virtuosity shown here is only the beginning of a pyrotechnic talent unfolding into the hidden dimensions of the human and nonhuman spirit."
-Jacqueline Lichtenberg

Set against a backdrop of contemporary culture, *Sons of Neverland* explores the universal questions of love, sex and death - the three most crucial challenges every human being must face. Stefan London is a grieving man, suffering through the loss of his young daughter. When he goes to a science fiction convention in the hopes of meeting her friends, he encounters instead a young man who is dangerously seductive and undeniably magical. Lured into the night, Stefan soon discovers himself in a place where vampires are real, and the world is not at all what he has always believed, and immortality is only a deep red kiss away.

But the price of eternal life is high, and as his handsome maker warns, "Through my blood you will learn a secret which will compel you to live forever, yet a secret so sinister it will haunt you for that same eternity."

The secret will haunt you, too.

———

"This book zones on the question of immortality. However, this is not just the decadent historical immortality of the long-lived vampire, it is immortality as a change in one's perception. This is the story behind the story, delivered by characters that are hyper-real - each one loaded with symbolism. *Sons of Neverland* will have you filled, even brimming over with the sense of Mysterium Tremendum et Fascinans. Go there for a full helping of the numinous." (A Reviewer on Amazon)

Also available in paperback on Amazon, or order from your favorite bookseller.

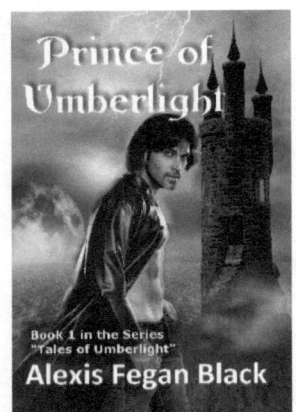

Prince of Umberlight
Alexis Fegan Black

"If <u>Prince of Umberlight</u> doesn't rattle your cage, you're more dead than the undead!" - **Night Readers**

Thorn may be an 800 year old vampire, but he does not possess the ability to create others of his kind, and so he is cursed to fall in love with mortals, only to watch them grow old and die. Torn by grief, Thorn denounces his immortality and enters into a comatose oblivion for decades.

When he awakens, he is no longer in London, but finds himself in a world spun into being by his own desires - a world where Time and Death do not exist, a world where it is forever autumn, where the Parish of Shadows and the River of Stars become his home. It is in this world of Umberlight that he meets Atom - an interloper into his private sanctuary, but also an impudent imp who is destined to reveal to Thorn the three dangerous elements a vampire must possess in order to become a Creator.

The Art of Brutality.
Submission to Dark Desire.
Love.

<u>Prince of Umberlight</u>

Also available in paperback on Amazon, or order from your favorite bookseller.

222

YEAR OF THE RAM
Della Van Hise

Year of the Ram was described by one reviewer as... "A space-faring male/male romance full of love, angst, and longing."

Only after Star Commander Morgan Diego becomes an exile as a result of a Galaxy Corps political blunder does he begin to realize how much he valued the companionship of his second in command - the mysterious Lucien, an Alfarian who is more elven than human, with peculiar powers & abilities which begin to unfold as he, too, realizes what he has lost.

Separated by circumstance from his former life, Morgan is thrust into a world where he must survive by his wits. When he meets a peculiar little old man calling himself Kim Le, Morgan finds himself in a situation where he is required to master The Art - not only a form of human & extraterrestrial martial arts, but a way of living and being that will alter his life forever.

At the temple, he is introduced to his new teacher, another Alfarian who begins to steal his heart - a heart which is already promised to Lucien. Torn and conflicted, Morgan struggles with the world he left behind and the world he now inhabits.

Beginning to believe he may never again return to his ship and to the friends and loved ones he left behind, he is all the more frustrated and heartbroken when a new Master arrives at the temple: a man to whom Morgan is immediately drawn both mentally and physically, a man who is strikingly familiar... yet utterly alien.

Year of the Ram is a fully-fleshed novel, approximately 97000 words, with a focus on the love story and romance angle. Set against a science fiction milieu, it explores the infinite possibilities of the human and alien heart. Sexual content is explicit, though is not the primary focus of the novel.

For those who like a romance that forces its characters to contemplate the ecstasies and the agonies of love... you will enjoy *Year of the Ram*.

Also available in paperback on Amazon,
or order from your favorite bookseller.

All of our titles are available directly from our website, on Amazon, or may be ordered from most booksellers. Thanks for reading us!

Eye Scry Publications
A Visionary Publishing Company
www.eyescrypublications.com